STEEL WOLF

EVE LANGLAIS

CHAPTER 1

TUNES ROCKED THE GARAGE AS I WORKED ON MY newest project: a 1958 Plymouth Fury. A sweet ride, most famous for being the psychotic car in Stephen King's thriller, *Christine*. I'd found the rusting—yet surprisingly good-condition—vehicle strategically buried under a mound of metal scrap at the back of my junkyard. Almost as if someone had wanted to hide it without causing too much damage.

I'd squealed louder than I ever did any Christmas morning when I uncovered it because it was mine. All mine. My divorce settlement from *The Jerk*—the only name suitable for my ex-husband—had bought and paid for the junkyard. Married for twenty-three years, starting right after we graduated college, where we'd dated on and off for two more. A good partnership for the most part until he hit his forties and suffered a midlife crisis that didn't just involve buying a sports car, getting hair plugs, and waxing his chest. It also came with a young girlfriend, who wanted the wife gone.

Me being the wife.

In a sense, I should thank The Jerk for freeing me from the most mind-numbingly boring existence on Earth. I'd not realized how much I hated my life until he told me I couldn't have it.

I celebrated by setting his shit on fire. The flames were really pretty, and I might have roasted marshmallows if the firemen hadn't ruined my fun.

In the end, I got the last laugh. Eric, a young stud of thirty to my forties, had stayed behind on the pretext of making sure none of the embers reignited. The only thing that caught fire was my pants, which he adeptly removed before showing off his hose skills.

Good time. And the only time Eric got to show me his hose. I wasn't looking for a full or even a part-time man. Didn't need one. What I *did* like was a good, hard fuck when the mood hit, something The Jerk couldn't manage, not without a bunch of prep and a pill.

Putting aside my grinder, I pushed up my goggles to eye the metal I'd been sanding to ensure I'd removed all the rust. Clean and smooth, or was that my aching shoulders talking?

I'd check it over tomorrow and buff any remaining spots before sending it to Danny, my custom paint guy, for a fresh, glossy look—color pending, despite the most obvious choice of red.

Did I want to be a copycat or give it a look that popped on its own merit? I'd have to decide soon.

If the parts I'd ordered arrived, I'd finish it and be able to put it up for sale within the month. Or I might keep it. After all, I didn't hurt for cash, and it spoke to me. *Drive me, Allie. You know you want to hear me roar.*

Hell, yeah, I did. I'd always loved cars—even from a young age when other girls played with Barbies. I'd only stopped playing with motors when I moved to Toronto with The Jerk. Big, expensive cities like Toronto came with some sacrifice, like no room to park a car to fix at my leisure. No time either, with my job clocking fifty hours of my life a week, plus the subway commute, which I hated.

If I never rode public transit again, I'd be just fine. Happy. Ecstatic, actually. Getting puked on once by the happy hour crowd was too much. It had happened three times.

Never again. I lived outside of Ottawa now, far enough away to avoid the congestion of people. And did what I loved.

I'd forgotten the calming pleasure of working with a beautiful vehicle. Of watching an old wreck return to the glory of its past.

Clang.

A frown creased my brow as something metallic crashed outside. Probably raccoons playing in the towers of metal again. Literally towers that defied gravity. I planned to compact and sell some of it to make room and reduce the hazards, but the crusher was waiting on parts, and had been since I'd bought the place. Showing the city inspectors my many emails asking the parts company when they'd arrive was the only thing keeping the city from fining me.

But they wouldn't be kind forever.

Jingle. Jangle. More tumbling metal. Were the raccoons fighting? I'd seen those furry, masked fiends get violent. Spats outside my bedroom window had woken me numerous times. Not the most pleasant thing since it resulted in barely any sleep as I hugged my shaking dog for the rest of the night. My fur baby didn't like strange and scary noises.

If the raccoons were fighting in the junkyard, at least they wouldn't be outside my house. Thinking of which, I should get to bed. I'd worked later than planned. I rolled my shoulders as I headed for the garage door. Past midnight, and my forty-seven-year-old ass would complain about it in the morning. Staying fit didn't make me immune to the effects of aging. I'd pop a few Tylenol and ignore it.

Before exiting, I shut off the switch that controlled the power for the garage—lights, outlets—which meant the radio abruptly silenced.

Outside, the night was quiet, and the yard mostly dark as the quarter-moon did little to illuminate the place. As for the motion sensor lights? The bulbs appeared to have burned out. Again. Had to be some kind of short because in the almost-year I'd owned the place, I'd replaced them three times already.

I heard a thump as I headed for the path to my house, situated conveniently next door to the junkyard. My head swiveled to the trailer I used as an office—a blocky rectangle with a few windows and a single door. I kept most of the junkyard paperwork, an old computer, and a safe inside—nothing of real value. Most of the transactions I processed were online and went right into an accounting program that handled everything for me. Locate the part requested, invoice, pick up by the client once they paid. I'd even deliver for a little extra.

My business did okay. I would probably need to do a bit of marketing to let people know of my existence. Place a few ads on Kiji and social media.

A sudden flare of light in my office trailer, followed by some noises, halted me and changed the direction of my feet. *Someone is fucking robbing me.*

They'd be disappointed. The office didn't have much to steal, but that didn't mean I'd let them get away with it.

"Fucking asshole. I'll teach you to fuck with my shit, you fucker," I swore. Fuck being a curse word I used often. Verb, adjective, noun. It fit into a lot of my speech these days. Call it catching up for the years I'd kept my words clean so as not to offend my husband, the uptight yuppy. It wasn't until after we'd split that I realized just how much I'd repressed the real me.

The real me being a beer-drinking, foul-mouthed, take-no-shit kind of girl. *I am woman. Hear me fucking roar.*

Whoever thought me an easy mark would get an earful before I handed them over to the cops for a proper eye-opener on their choices in life.

I pulled out my cell phone as I headed for the building but hesitated. Did I really want to call the cops? That would involve talking to someone, maybe even going down to the station to fill out a report. Getting home around dawn.

Ugh.

On second thought, I'd just scare the piss out of the person in my office. I had a barrel of rebar rods sitting next to the office trailer. I grabbed one of the shorter ones. If the intruder got frisky, I'd give them a few whacks, enough to show that I meant business.

Light spilled from the entrance to my office as the door stood ajar. Not even trying to hide.

I stepped in to see a skinny dude with a nose ring rifling through my desk.

"What the fuck do you think you're doing, asshole?" I pointed my weapon and waved it menacingly.

Bloodshot eyes rose from the drawer to me. The lip curled upward. "Where's the money, bitch?"

I arched a brow. "Big words for a little man."

"Not that little." When he rose from his crouch, he stood taller than me, but heavy drug use had emaciated him. His features were drawn tight; his eyes streaked red and sickly looking in the fluorescent lighting. His short sleeves showed the bruised and splotched flesh where he injected his arms.

A druggie, tweaking hard—jonesing for his next hit. Needing cash and desperate for it. "Leave. Now. There's no money."

"Liar! Hand over the cash, and you won't get hurt." He came around the side of the desk, and I retreated to the door. I wanted to lure him outside to give myself more room to swing.

"Go find another place to rob." I stood in

the doorway, rod extended, debating if I should run or not.

Someone punching the back of my knee and sending me tumbling took that decision from me.

Only in that moment did I realize that the tweaker hadn't come alone.

CHAPTER 2

As I BUCKLED AND FELL TO THE GROUND, A punch to the head knocked me sideways. Before I could recover, the second thief wrenched the rod from my hand.

I popped to my feet and whirled in time to take a closed fist to the face. I reeled, stumbling hard enough that I lost my balance and hit the ground again, hard, the breath knocked out of me, my brains scrambled. The intruders stood on either side of me, their shapes blurring from two to four.

"Where's the money, cunt?" The guy who'd stolen my rod stood over me, menacing. He wore a dark hoodie and had a bit more heft to his frame than his friend.

At that point, even I knew better than to

fight over cash. "Desk drawer, under the receipt tray. There's only a bit of petty cash."

Skinny ran back inside and then re-emerged, waving a handful of bills. "Found it!"

Hefty didn't appear impressed. "That's just a decoy. I'll bet she's got more stashed." He jabbed my belly with the end of the rod. "Where's the rest?"

"That's all of it."

"Liar!" The whack of the bar drew a sharp gasp of pain.

Before Hefty could swing again, I grabbed the metal rod. We tugged, back and forth. I lost, no match for drugged, adrenaline-fueled strength. He ripped the rod from my hands, splitting open my left palm.

The sight of the blood widened Skinny's eyes. "We should get out of here."

His friend didn't agree. "Not before she coughs up the cash. Where is it?"

"I have no more money."

"Lying cunt!" He swung.

I raised my arm in time to block the blow. Sharp pain made me wonder if he'd broken my arm. I rolled before he could strike again and popped to my feet.

"Joey. Stop. We got enough for a hit." Skinny tried to stop his buddy.

"Says you. I think she's got enough hidden for more than a measly pinch each."

As they argued, I saw my chance and ran, gritting my teeth against the pain. The eye he'd punched had already swollen shut. My arm throbbed. More of me would hurt if I didn't escape, though. Fear hastened my steps. Like any wounded prey, I looked for a spot to hide. While I'd owned the junkyard for almost a year now, I'd not gone through even a quarter of the towers of junk. I'd been taking my time dismantling the piles to unearth the treasures: old cars and appliances. If it had metal and a motor, chances were, it ended up in the junkyard. Then I tagged it, took a picture, and uploaded it to my website. Once the search engines indexed it, anyone looking could find me.

I headed for one of the untouched mounds.

I didn't make it.

The sudden pounding of footsteps at my rear barely prepared me. I spun around. Too late. Once more, the one called Joey clobbered me.

Stunned, I couldn't avoid the sweep of my ankles that dumped me onto the ground.

The hefty Joey, grinning and showing off his black and tartar-covered teeth, stood over me. "Either hand over the cash, or I'll take my payment in flesh." He leered.

I gagged. The thought of him touching me… I'd rather die.

His companion arrived and shoved him. "Joey, enough. We got the money. Let's go."

"Not before I get me some action." His hands went to his pants, held up by a knotted shoestring.

"Gross, dude. Leave the old hag alone."

Old? I took offense, even as I crawled away.

A hand grabbed me by the ankle. "Where do you think you're going?"

Desperate, I reached out to grab hold of something, anything, to stem the drag back into the Hell Joey promised. My fingers clamped around metal, and I clung for dear life as my assailant pulled and laughed.

"Feisty, I like it," he chortled.

Sick fucker. I didn't let go, but my grip grew slippery from the blood oozing from the slice across my palm. It smeared the metal I'd chosen as my anchor, making it harder and harder to hold on.

A hard yank tore me free, and I couldn't help but scream, "Fuck off!" as I kicked and thrashed.

As if the would-be rapist listened.

Joey flipped me over, and even in the gloom, I saw him lick his lips in anticipation. He dropped to his knees, pinning me in place. I shoved at him, but dizzy and in pain, he easily batted aside my hands. It didn't help that his friend had changed his mind and chose to restrain my left arm.

I wanted to cry but could only pray. *Please, help me.*

Please.

The mountain of metal looming over us groaned and uttered a metallic squeal as it shifted.

"That didn't sound good. Maybe we should move." Joey's nervous friend released my arm.

"You're right. We should relocate. The office had a soft-looking couch," Joey agreed a second before a hunk of metal came crashing down, knocking him aside. Before I could move, the mountain of junk fell over, knocking me out cold.

CHAPTER 3

I WASN'T SURE HOW LONG I LOST CONSCIOUSNESS. All I knew was that when I woke, I found myself pinned under a pile of metal, still wearing my pants and not throbbing anywhere I shouldn't. The more pressing question, though: Had the tweakers left?

I barely dared to breathe as I listened. I certainly didn't move. Hearing nothing, I tried to assess my situation. Dire, despite the fact that I'd escaped being raped and killed. I appeared to be under a mound of junk, a sizeable one, with no idea how to get free.

In some astonishing piece of luck, despite the mountain that'd fallen on me, it didn't appear as if it had crushed any part of my body. However, the detritus *did* surround me in a cage that I didn't dare shift, out of fear that I'd upset the precarious balance that kept me from being squashed flat like a bug.

It would be the height of irony if my midlife dream occupation ended up being the death of me. I could see the headline now: *Woman found eaten by raccoons under a pile of scrap metal. Neighbors express surprise that it wasn't cats, given she was an almost fifty-year-old divorcee.*

In reality, no one would give a shit if I died. Most of my friends had drifted away over the years. Some had moved for jobs. Others because of their partners. But the majority had split off when they had babies. They'd become families who did family things.

I preferred a dog. One who would be worried when his mama didn't come home.

While I couldn't see anything, I *could* move my hands and pulled forth the phone I should have used before. I'd been brash and stupid, confronting those intruders. In my defense, this should have been a safe place. Drug crimes usually flourished in the downtown areas, not out in the boonies where I had chosen to do business.

It took some maneuvering before I could

dial.

"Nine-one-one, what's your emergency?"

"I was attacked."

The tone turned brisk and efficient. "Where are you? Are you injured?"

"Definitely bruised. I don't know if anything is broken. I can't really move as I'm stuck under a pile of junk."

"Er, what?" The surprise in the operator's voice almost made me smile.

Only there wasn't anything funny about the situation.

I quickly explained and gave them my location. I would have stayed on the line if my phone hadn't died. Not really a surprise. Usually, I charged it overnight.

As I lay there, I tried not to panic, especially since a cold breeze tickled my skin. It didn't help that I had the sense of being watched. *Please, don't let it be rats.* I fucking hated those pink-tailed bastards.

It felt like an eternity before I heard the sirens. Never thought I'd be happy to see the cops. Although, the time it took to bust open the lock to the main gates tempered that happiness.

Not knowing if they could see me, I started

yelling. "I'm over here."

"Found her. I see feet," someone yelled, flashing a light that blinded me through the crevices formed by the metal tenting over me.

"Hold on, ma'am. We're figuring out how to extract you without destabilizing the pile."

Being a bit of a smart ass, I quipped, "Anyone bring the jaws of life?"

I was worried when a different voice whispered, "Should we go get them?"

But it turned out they only had one real idiot in the group. The rest of the officers proved efficient, setting up lights and then playing a game of Jenga with my metal tent.

They removed pieces one by one, being careful not to shift the weight of the pile on me. It took forever, and only as they got to the last layer covering me did I see what had kept me from being crushed—an old motorcycle frame. The thick handlebars on the front dug into the ground and angled the body, allowing it to hold everything else off me. As the first responders heaved the last bits from me, I emerged like a broken butterfly from her metal cocoon to rapid-fire questions. The cops' faces were a blur, as were the EMTs' surrounding me.

"Are you okay?"

"Can you tell us what happened?"

"Where does it hurt?"

I gave them the condensed version of my attack while an EMT placed a blanket around my shoulders. I'd not realized just how cold I'd gotten lying there. The same EMT tried to get me on a stretcher, but I waved her off.

"I'm fine," I protested as I tottered for the flashing lights in the main part of my yard. It might have been more convincing if I hadn't passed out.

I woke in a hospital bed, which, depending on your purview, wasn't necessarily better than the pile of junk. I'd always hated hospitals. The smell. The noise. I'd spent too much time inside one as my mom battled cancer—two years of watching the woman who loved me waste away. At least my dad had gone quickly. A heart attack that'd dropped him instantly.

A quick assessment showed an IV in my arm, most likely fluids so I didn't dehydrate. Too many bandages adorned my body, including one around my temple and over one eye. Judging by my pain level, they'd definitely not drugged me heavily enough. The slightest movement brought a gasp to my lips. Still, determined, I heaved myself into a sitting position.

My one good eye closed to fight the spinning in my head, which meant I didn't realize that I wasn't alone until a man spoke.

"Mrs. Collins-Harris, are you awake?"

The old name brought a curl to my lips. "Actually, it's Ms. Collins. I'm divorced." Sadly, not all my identification showed it yet. Funny how the government had no problem changing my name to add The Jerk's surname, but when taking it off, they dragged their bureaucratic feet.

It shouldn't be that difficult. After all, I'd existed before I married The Jerk. I'd brought in just as much as he did to the household. But, apparently, that didn't count for shit. Citing delays from a pandemic long over, I'd yet to receive my updated health card and driver's license.

"Ms. Collins, I am sorry to intrude, but I was hoping you might be feeling well enough to answer some questions."

"Do I look like someone in the mood to chat?" I replied sourly. My pasty mouth felt as if something had crawled in and died. My one unbandaged eye remained closed and gummy. Pretty girl. *Not.* "If you're looking for a news story, bug someone else." Damned reporters, always trying to make a buck off someone's misery.

"Actually, I'm Detective Walker with the Ontario Provincial Police."

"Lucky me, rating a visit from the OPP," I drawled as I squinted open my one good eye, immediately wishing I'd kept it closed.

I would, of course, look like shit—that had been stomped flat, baked in the sun, then scraped off the sidewalk—when confronted by a hunk of a detective—blond-haired, blue-eyed, with a chiseled jaw. And I'd bet those shoulders were naturally broad. As for the laugh lines at the corners of his eyes, indicating a fellow in his forties, at least? Only made him sexier.

"Given your property borders Highway 7, criminal offenses fall under our jurisdiction."

"If you say so. Don't really care." I really didn't. What I wanted was for the pounding in my head to go away. "Grab a nurse on your way out, would you? And tell them to bring me some Tylenol."

"A moment." He moved to the door and

stuck his head out, the deep murmur showing that he spoke to someone. When he turned around, he offered me a smile. "A nurse is checking with the doctor to see if it's okay first. Says she'll be a few minutes. Enough time for us to chat."

"Not in the mood," I grouched.

"I realize that. And I'm sorry to be disturbing you, given your obvious trauma. However, I'd like to catch those responsible for the attack before they hurt anyone else."

Ah, the good ol' guilt trip. I sighed. "Meaning, you haven't nabbed the fuckers already."

"Usually, we need a name or a description before we arrest folks."

I snorted. "As if that will make a difference. You guys tend to be bleeding hearts where tweakers are concerned."

"Only until they prove themselves to be a menace."

"Is that why I rated a detective? Because they escalated from petty crime to trying to murder me?"

"Did they try to kill you?"

"Does it matter? Fact is, they beat the shit out of me and planned to rape me. The only reason we're talking now is because I got buried under some junk instead of being tortured to death."

"I saw the photos from the scene. It's a miracle you survived. You're a very lucky woman."

That made me laugh, which hurt. My ribs let me know I'd not escaped unscathed. "Not feeling so lucky right now."

"Let's fix that. Help me find the perpetrators."

"Listen, Detective, while I appreciate you coming here to see me in the hospital, there's not much I can actually tell you. The guys jumped me when I went to check on my office because I saw a light and heard some noise."

"Can you describe them?"

"Yeah." He took notes as I detailed what I remembered, including the name: *Joey.*

"Do you recall anything else? Tattoos? Scars? Birthmarks?"

"Other than the skinny one's nose ring, nothing else. Everything happened so fast."

"You said you saw and heard them. You live on the premises?"

I nodded. "Next door. But I wasn't actually in my house. I was working late on a project in the garage."

"You own the junkyard?" He checked his notebook. "Bits and Bolts?"

"Yup." I'd bought it when I needed a fresh start. A divorce hadn't been enough. When my husband dropped his bombshell, I'd needed to go somewhere new. Do something different.

"I want kids." A declaration The Jerk had made out of the blue after we'd always stated that we would never have any.

"I don't." Never saw the appeal. Snotty, whiny little critters, constantly demanding attention. Let other people have them. I was perfectly happy with our dog.

"Come on, wouldn't you like a kid to pass on your legacy?"

At the time, I had to snort. I was working as a receptionist for a car dealership. "What legacy? And where is this coming from? We agreed we didn't want any." For going on twenty years.

"I changed my mind."

"Well, I haven't." And at my age, I really wasn't interested. I'd thought that was the end of it.

It was the end, just not the one I'd expected. He hit me with divorce papers and the news that his much younger girlfriend was pregnant.

In retrospect, I might not have handled things well. After I set his shit on fire, I'd had his BMW towed to a chop shop for parts. Bad of me, I know. Yet the judge forgave me when the bastard had the balls to show up in court with his super-pregnant girlfriend.

Despite The Jerk's wishes, the judge split everything down the middle—as was fair. We'd both made pretty much the same salary, so The Jerk could shove his snotty attitude.

I got half of all our assets, which meant a nice chunk of cash, given that our house sold during the pandemic for way over asking price. The housing market had blown up in Southern Ontario as people sought more space.

Needing a fresh start, I'd moved out of the Golden Horseshoe area in Ontario to just out-side a small town, a good four hours away from my old life. Carleton Place. With the di-vorce proceeds, I'd bought myself a derelict business formerly called Steel Deals—a junk-yard abandoned when the owner disappeared more than a decade earlier. Rumor claimed he'd run from the cops. I didn't care. The town had taken ownership due to unpaid taxes, and I'd picked it up for a song at auction. Even bet-ter, it'd come with a house attached to the property.

A home that required some major renovation to truly make it livable, but I didn't mind. Adrift and alone for the first time in forever, I'd needed to keep busy. And keep busy I did: painting, redoing floors, cleaning up the plumbing, and testing the electrical. I'd always been a handy girl—blame my father, who'd wanted a boy. Dad might have died of a heart attack when I was twenty-two, but I remembered everything he taught me. I found peace in getting my hands dirty.

I expected the detective to make some sexist remark. Most men did once they found out I owned a junkyard.

Instead, he said, "Have you had any problems since you took ownership?"

"Nope. Usually pretty quiet, day and night." I'd not yet seen much traffic, probably because I'd not really advertised the reopening.

"Do you know how much money was in your office?"

"Maybe thirty or forty bucks." I shrugged and fought a wince. "Most people pay by credit card or debit. Bigger purchases, they transfer the funds via email money transfer."

"You were alone when it happened?"

"Why, Detective, are you trying to find out if I'm single?" I drawled.

"Are you?"

Given I likely looked like a truck had run me over, I doubted he was flirting. Despite the lack of a ring on his finger, a good-looking guy like him probably had a partner.

Not that it mattered. Even if he were available, I didn't date. Since the divorce, I'd stuck to one-night-stand fucking. Being single didn't mean I wanted a vibrator taking care of me all the time when the mood hit. I think that was what'd killed me about my ex. Up until the day before he announced the divorce, we were still having sex. For fuck's sake, he'd had his face between my legs that very morning. He might not have a reliable penis, but the man worked his tongue.

"I live alone. Which reminds me, did anybody go inside my house? I've got a dog, and he's scared of strangers." I'd adopted Blade at a shelter years ago—some kind of mixed breed with black fur. At one hundred and forty pounds, he looked like a vicious bastard, who might be part wolf. In reality? He was the world's biggest pussy. It wasn't just people that frightened him. The dark sent him hiding. Thunderstorms. Fireworks. Using the blender usually had him tucked under the kitchen table, shaking.

While Blade didn't mind the junkyard in the daytime, he hated it at night. The first time I'd taken him there after dark, he'd gotten so scared, he'd bolted into the towers of metal. Took forever to coax him out, and even longer before he stopped shaking. Out of concern for his safety—and because rocking a massive dog for two hours in my lap cut into my sleep—I now left him home when I worked late, and installed a doggy door that led into a secure dog run for him to do his business.

"Your dog should be secure. Since the crime occurred in your office and outside, there was no need to enter the premises."

"Good." The last time I'd had a stranger in the house to hook up my cable, Blade had hidden under my bed. Which would have been fine if he'd not gotten stuck. I'd had to jack my frame to get him out.

"Since we're on the topic of your home, would you mind if I visited you, perhaps tomorrow, to show you some mug shots?" The detective had yet to pull out a notebook and take any notes.

"You think they're repeat offenders?"

"I'd say it's a distinct possibility, given it's a known pattern with petty crime."

"Because Ontario's soft on criminals," I grumbled. "And I wouldn't call what they did to me petty."

"I agree. Hence why we should locate them, given the gravity of their attempt. "

"And if you find them? Then what? They spend a few months in jail and get dumped back on the streets."

His lips thinned. "Possibly. I'm afraid we're at the mercy of the laws and the judges."

"The laws suck." Because they allowed scum to keep victimizing.

"So?"

"So, what?" I snapped.

"May I visit you to show you those pictures?"

"Yeah. I guess." Maybe I'd get lucky, and they'd actually find the fuckers. But I wouldn't hold my breath, or I'd most likely die. "If I'm not at the house, you'll probably find me in the garage, working on a wreck."

"You rebuild cars?"

"I do now." I'd worked night and day on my first—a restored Trans Am with the famous Firebird on the hood—and sold it faster than expected. The Plymouth would be my third.

"Odd profession for a woman."

Aha, he finally showed his true colors. I pounced. "Kind of a sexist thing to say in this day and age."

"I agree, but in my defense, I've never met a woman mechanic."

"We're the same as guys, only without dicks."

His lips quirked. "I'd say there's more to you than that."

"What can I say? I'm a woman of many surprises."

"Speaking of surprises, have you thought of adding security to avoid unexpected visitors?"

"No. Didn't think I had to." But the attack had made it clear I'd have to do *something*.

"I can refer you to someone if you need a hand with that."

"Not going to volunteer yourself?" Yup, I definitely flirted that time. And got shot down as he stood.

"Thank you for your time, Ms. Collins. I'll be in touch."

I knew what I'd like him to touch once the rest of me stopped hurting.

CHAPTER 4

THE DETECTIVE LEFT, AND A NURSE CAME IN right after to take my vitals. Two hours later, after the nurse had promised the doctor would be right in, he finally arrived.

"Ms. Collins. You're a very lucky lady!" he announced. Apparently, despite my aches and many contusions, I would recover. Nothing was broken. I didn't appear to have internal injuries. Even my eye should be fine, I just needed to give it a few days for the swelling to go down.

With all that good news—excuse the fucking sarcasm—I was told I could go. The revolving door of Canadian healthcare at its best. They'd probably already stripped my bed and prepped it for the next wham-bam-thank-you client in the medical system.

I could only hope they'd not missed anything vital as I limped my ass out of there, getting all kinds of looks as I only had my cruddy and bloody jeans and sweatshirt to wear. My clothes were less of a problem than my lack of wallet and cash. No charging cord meant my phone remained dead, and I had no means of getting home. Standing in the lobby of the hospital, I wanted to cry.

This was what I got for moving away from the city I'd grown up in. No friends I could call because I'd not exactly been Mrs. Social since arriving in Ottawa. No family. Just me and my two feet, one of which dragged from the bruising on my hip.

I sat in a hard plastic chair as I tried to figure out what to do.

Which was how Detective Walker found me. "Need a ride?"

The detective offered me a much-needed lift. But could I be courteous and grateful? Nope. Suspicion reared its head. "Why are you still here?"

"Dealing with another case."

"What kind of case?"

"The kind that's none of your business."

My lips almost curved until I realized that smiling wouldn't improve my grotesque appearance. Meaning, his offer likely had nothing to do with him hitting on me. Unless he liked his women all beaten up. "My mother taught me to never accept a ride from a stranger."

"Hardly strangers, given you know my name and where to find me. So, one last time, do you want a ride?"

My lips parted, readying to utter an emphatic, "*no*." Only an idiot would accept a ride from a cop. Still, I didn't have many options unless I stole someone's charging cord and got enough juice to order a rideshare. The effort involved daunted. "You sure? I'm probably out of your way."

"You are." He didn't deny it. "But you look like you could use a break."

"Aren't you still on the work clock?"

"Yes. And your attack is one of my cases."

The relegation to a duty he had to perform soured me.

Why? Why did I care? Yes, he was cute. About my age, with sandy blond hair that either hid the gray well or meant he had none. His age only became apparent in the deeper creases around his eyes and inset within his forehead.

Broad shoulders in an open jacket and dress shirt that didn't appear to stretch over his abdomen but *did* get tight around the top part of his chest, the top two buttons undone.

I really should stop staring and say something. "Are you a perv?"

Blunt, and yet being direct sometimes worked best. Catch them unaware.

"I am not going to molest you on the way home, if that's what you're asking."

"Says you."

"I have a dashcam we can use to record the trip."

Sounded great in theory until I remembered one, how I looked, and two... "I don't want everything I say to be recorded." Because what if something stupid slipped out? I could get awkward when flustered. And right now counted.

"Are you coming or not?" Other men might have said this with much impatience, but Detective Walker remained steady and oozed trustworthiness.

I had to remind myself that The Jerk hadn't started out that way. I'd gotten a good twenty years out of him. Many of them dull, in retro-spect. Yet, I shared some of that blame.

All that to say, my man-dar worked per-fectly fine. The Jerk and I had just grown apart. If my intuition said the detective wasn't an ass-hole, then I should listen to it—and stop eye-balling him as a potential dick.

Since being single, I had a tendency to filter every comment and action made by an attrac-tive male into a few categories. Flirting, not flirting, orgasm potential, or run away—fast and hard.

The detective fell into the bad-idea cate-gory, but I needed a ride home. Before I could overthink it even more, I rose and said, "I'd love a ride."

I hadn't meant for it to emerge salaciously. A good thing he didn't pick up on it.

"I'm parked a few minutes' walk away."

His idea of a few minutes happened at a fast clip. With my bruised body, I managed a lopsided hitching gait at best. It led to him shortening and slowing his stride.

"Nice day," he remarked, as I wished I had sunglasses to choke out the bright sunlight.

I'd been working a lot at night with the flu-orescents on. In the daytime, I sometimes opened the large bay door; however, the sun never hit it the right way to truly light up the inside.

All to say, I might be part vampire. I certainly wanted to suck on the guy by my side.

It was the last thing I should be thinking of, and yet the only thing strong enough to distract me from the discomfort of my body. I could have used a massage.

I eyed the detective's hands. Big, but the fingers didn't appear too callused. A glance farther down showed his feet a good size. Promising. The step off the curb, and the ensuing jab of pain after, shoved that thought right out of my head.

Ouch.

I might have uttered a complaint aloud because he murmured, "Almost there."

The detective drove a sedan—a boring, dark-colored four-door that smelled of fake pine needles when we got in. Not a piece of garbage could be seen. Not even a Timmy's coffee cup.

Impressive. Movies and shows always portrayed detectives as the biggest slobs. Lucky me, I'd found a hot one who wasn't an actual pig—explained why he didn't once look at me.

He probably saw me as trash. I'd seen it growing up. As a girl who liked boyish things but dressed kind of slutty, people made many assumptions. That I was easy to fuck. Tough in a fight.

The truth being, The Jerk was only the second guy I'd ever been with. As for going toe-to-toe with someone? Not for a long while. But that might be changing. The lady in the grocery store who'd plucked a box of bakery-fresh cookies out of my shopping cart had almost gotten throat punched.

"Hey, what are you doing?" I'd exclaimed in surprise. *"Those were in my cart."*

"I need them more than you. Some of us have kids."

I glanced at her cart with its eclectic grouping of food, easily microwaveable pizza pockets, chips, cereal more sugar than nutrition, flavored crystals, and my cookies. "Your kids need you to talk to a nutritionist. Look at all that crap."

The lady gaped at me. "How dare you?"

"No, how dare you?" I snatched back my cookies. *"Think of this as a good time to learn how to bake with your demon spawn. Maybe something with a vegetable or fruit in it."*

In that moment, in that grocery store, I'd

stood up for myself, something I'd not done in years because I didn't want to rock the boat.

It occurred to me that the detective hadn't said a word since we'd left the hospital. I'd expected a few questions about my attack. Instead, he kept his focus on the road, played some soft jazz on the radio that I didn't totally hate, and not once tried to put his hand on my thigh.

As he drove past my junkyard, I noticed the gates wide open. Fuck me. Why not put out a sign inviting people to rob me blind? Then again, so long as they didn't take the stuff in my garage, would I really notice a wreck missing from the many piles?

Despite me not saying a word, the detective knew to turn into the driveway next to the fenced-in yard and then pulled to a stop in front of my tiny bungalow. Weathered, light blue siding, a metal roof a brighter shade of blue—utterly hideous and likely to last forever —and old-style windows framed in wood instead of PVC. They sucked in the cold weather, but I loved the look of them, so I'd counter by eventually adding solar to power the heated floors I'd install.

From the outside? Pure shithole. I'd yet to

decide if I'd bother to change it. Let people misjudge the contents. I'd been working on the interior when I wasn't fixing the cars and uploading random parts online. I really needed to get to sorting the junk faster. Then I could sell the scrap that I couldn't use and start taking in new wrecks.

"How do you like living here?" the detective asked suddenly as I reached for the handle to escape the sedan.

My one shoulder lifted and fell. "It's all right. The Ottawa Valley is a lot quieter than I'm used to."

"I meant the junkyard and house. No problems with the ghost?"

I blinked at him. "What ghost?"

His lips curved, and hot damn, look at that. A dimple. It remained as he spoke. "People say the guy who used to own this place didn't actually skip town but rather died and has been haunting the junkyard ever since."

I snorted. "Please. Don't tell me you believe in that malarky."

He shrugged. "I don't. But we've had a few calls over the years from people claiming they saw and heard things."

"What kinds of things?"

"If I tell you, then you'll really think I'm nuts." His smile widened.

Despite the pain in my face, I couldn't help but return it. "Well, I hate to break it to you, but I haven't run into any poltergeist activity, strange moans, or unidentified floating sheets."

"If you do, call me." He handed me a card, which I grabbed before pulling on the door handle.

"Okay. Thanks again for the ride."

"My pleasure, Ms. Collins."

"Call me Allie." Which was short for Alyssa. But he probably already knew that.

"I'll see you soon, Allie." Said with low promise before he drove off.

I watched him get back onto Highway 7—my business was on a less-frequented section of the popular road—and wondered if I'd imagined him flirting. He was probably just the kind of guy who talked like that to every-one. Part of his cop training to put people at ease so they spilled their guts. Since I had nothing to admit, I was more likely to drop my pants.

Yup. Despite being bruised and battered, my midlife libido remained fully operational.

And it wanted the detective.

CHAPTER 5

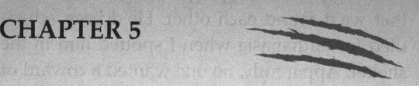

I LIMPED INTO THE HOUSE, USING THE HIDE-A-KEY I kept stashed in the porch light. I whistled. "Blade? Where are you, baby?"

Probably hiding because someone dared to enter. But upon hearing my voice, high-pitched crying emerged from deeper in the house before resolving into a giant fluffball barreling at me.

Blade was what you'd get if you crossed a wolf with a Border Collie. In other words, large and really fucking hairy. Scared of everything, but he loved me.

He cried and danced around me, his massive tail swinging. Given it had knocked over light furniture before, I eschewed a front hall side table for a shelf higher than his tail of wagging destruction for my key bowl.

I hugged his wiggling body, glad once more that we'd found each other. He'd been scheduled for euthanasia when I spotted him in the shelter. Apparently, no one wanted a coward of his size. It was love at first sight. Those big eyes of his, the way he leaned on me with such trust.

The Jerk hadn't been impressed. He'd wanted a dog of breeding. Something with a fancy name and a pedigree. Me? I wanted sloppy kisses and pee on my feet. Blade had excitement issues.

It was why I kept Lysol wipes on the shelf alongside the bowl for my keys. I wiped the tops of my boots and floor, and with my happy furball by my side, headed for the kitchen where I disposed of them in the garbage can under the sink.

"Who's a hungry puppy?" Yes, there was irony in calling the hundred-and-forty-pound furball a puppy. Yet, even after three years together, Blade still possessed the sweet innocence that had drawn me to him.

The suggestion of food got more dancing and crying. Because while Blade had a dispenser for dry kibble, he loved treats. Hot Rods, to be exact. I gave him an entire stick, and he raced to his bed to lick it before scarfing it down.

While he made slobbery love to his favorite treat, I showered. I needed the smell of hospital and blood, and the memory of my attackers, gone from my skin. I stood under the steaming hot water so long that I boiled a shade only slightly lighter than cooked lobster. All the water in the world couldn't fix the bruises turning all kinds of hideous shades, but it did help my mental state.

Once I'd toweled off, I dressed in black track pants and my favorite red hoodie before padding out to my living room and staring blankly at my couch and television.

Sit and watch the boob tube or...my gaze strayed to the window. Before I could think twice, I'd slipped on my Crocs. I whistled. "Blade, you coming?"

Given it was daylight outside, my dog trotted alongside me as we crossed over to the junkyard using the shortcut that went from my side door to a gate in the fence. As I pulled on the latch, it occurred to me that I should probably get a lock for it. Not that it would make a difference. My front yard was unfenced, not to mention, I'd had the main gates barred the night of my attack. Meaning, those fuckers had probably climbed or already knew of my secret entrance.

I began to see the merit in barbed wire. Maybe a trench with spikes. A drone armed with rubber bullets. I glanced down at Blade. "I don't suppose I could put a spiked collar on you and convince you to look menacing?"

His tongue lolled as he grinned at me.

I sighed. Terrifying, he was not.

The first thing I did upon entering was head to the main gates and close them. As I eyed the busted lock—because, of course, the cops had to smash their way in—I pursed my lips. At the very least, I should invest in some new motion-sensor lights and cameras. Then, if someone dared to invade my place again, I'd have warning. Which made me wonder... should I get a gun? I'd never fired one, but maybe I should look into getting my license and lessons.

The attack had shaken me. That feeling of helplessness. The terror. The fact that I'd almost died, and they'd wanted to—

But didn't, I reminded myself firmly.

Despite it being the middle of the afternoon, I glanced around suspiciously as if the assholes might be lurking. I practically bolted for my workshop and grabbed a heavy metal wrench, which had Blade eyeing me with his head tilted.

"Just in case, baby." I felt better with its weight in my hand.

The car I'd been working on remained as I'd left it, but I didn't feel any excitement looking at it. I feared I'd forever associate it with my attack.

Speaking of attack... I wandered back outside, suspicious, cautious, ready to swing my mighty wrench. Fuck Thor and his hammer, this modern girl had her own weapon and a slobbery dog.

Blade pranced in the afternoon sunlight, chasing a passing bumblebee. Goofy idiot.

My smile at his antics faded as I headed for the office and noticed the police tape over the door. They'd dusted the place, which was more than I'd expected, given how little the tweakers had stolen. It didn't look any messier than usual, so I left it and wandered back outside, stopping short as I saw the dark spots on the ground. A chill hit me in an all-body tremble.

That's my blood. My scabbed lip throbbed—a reminder of the violence. Despite the tremor within and the fear, I retraced my steps until I stood by the scattered remains of metal. The once-impressive tower was now a toppled mess. The cops had left some evidence of their presence. Footprints in the dirt. A discarded evidence bag. From the way the junk framed an open spot, I could see where I'd lain on the ground. If I'd not woken and called for help, it would have been my cairn.

I knelt in the cleared area and took a moment to close my eyes and breathe. *Thank you, whatever god kept me safe.*

Or should I be giving thanks to the scrapped motorcycle that'd taken the brunt of the weight and thus saved me from being crushed? I still didn't understand how I'd gotten so lucky.

The cops who'd removed the bike hadn't been gentle and had let it fall to the side. Moving to the old frame, I crouched and ran my finger along its solid body. A jolt of electricity had me sucking in a breath.

What the fuck?

I glanced at the sky. Not a cloud in sight. Weird, but then again, metal was a conductor.

Curious, I grabbed the bike and stood it from the debris for a better look.

I didn't recognize the make or model. The frame bore a strange design, angling in a way I'd never encountered. The wheels had long gone flat, and the seat was torn with the stuffing gone. But it did still have an engine under the side plating, stroked in lines that reminded me of ruffled fur. The front of it—I squinted with my one good eye—was it me, or did that front end kind of look like a wolf's head?

"Grrr."

The noise startled me enough that I whipped my head around and then gaped in surprise as my dog—my floofy coward—crouched with his teeth bared in a growl.

"What's wrong, baby?" I glanced around and saw nothing.

Blade went from throaty noises to taking a step toward me, only to stop with a whine.

I glanced down at the bike. "Is this what's scaring you?" I shook it, and my dog barked before retreating several steps.

"It's just a hunk of metal."

Blade remained unconvinced and kept a wide berth as I rolled the bike back to my workshop. I'd admit to being intrigued and muttered aloud...

"Who made you? You're awfully unique. Why would anyone have abandoned you?" This kind of custom work wasn't cheap. And, no, it wasn't weird that I started talking to it. I always had the best conversations with my dog and inanimate objects. They never yapped back or called me old and cold.

I wasn't cold. I just didn't want kids.

Bringing the bike inside, I propped it against my workbench before going over it, looking for any identification. There wasn't any. No serial number. No vehicle identification number. No stamp indicating the builder. Nothing.

Whoever had built it had done so as a true custom. I had to wonder what it would fetch if I rebuilt it.

After I finished the Plymouth. *Never start a project unless you've finished one.* My mom's rule. Because, otherwise, our entire property would have held wrecks.

Despite my bruises, I spent the rest of that afternoon poring over the body of the car, making sure I'd not missed any spots. Blade slept in his bed by the side door, snoring loudly. A warning system of sorts if anyone arrived. While he wouldn't actually defend me, his running to hide while possibly whining would alert me to someone's presence. He didn't budge, other than to fart.

The roll-up door let in daylight and gave me a wide view of anyone approaching. No one did, and yet I remained distracted. My gaze kept popping over to the bike.

I used to ride back in my early twenties before I met The Jerk and became the wife of a lawyer, the kind who sat in an office all day filing real estate paperwork and said it wasn't seemly for me to act like some biker chick. The irony being that part of his midlife crisis had involved him getting a crotch rocket. Fucker. How did I not see before just how much I'd given up pretending to be his perfect trophy?

No more. At forty-seven, I still had plenty of time to live my best life. To do what I wanted. And what I wanted was to not be afraid. Tell that to my sudden anxiety as the sun started to sink in the sky.

"Come on, Blade. Let's go make some dinner." I kept my heavy wrench in hand as the roll-down door rattled in its track as it shut.

The wrench stayed in my sweaty grip as

Blade and I went out the side door. Given Blade sauntered out yawning, I figured I was safe. Tell that to my feet that had me hurrying to the front gate, where I locked it with the chain and spare padlock I'd dug out. Then I bolted to my house, the hide-a-key now permanently in my pocket. I didn't want to leave any way in.

Once inside, I locked the door and stared at it as Blade sauntered off. Then I glanced at the laundry room where he had his doggy door to the outside. Big enough to admit a slim person. Would those guys who attacked me fit? Hefty Joey wouldn't, but Slim might.

I shook my head. No. I wouldn't let my anxiety make me freak out. The chances of them coming back were slim. Like the cops had said, it was a crime of opportunity with little payout. Why would they come back?

"Who's a hungry boy?" I crooned and basked in my dog's love as he watched me adoringly while I made dinner. We ate together in the kitchen. He so loved fish and chips night. He got a plate of his own on the floor because I did have limits, and watching him eat with slobber and dropped pieces that got re-gobbled, pushed them.

After dinner, I settled on the couch with my tablet and went internet surfing, looking for the bike. Surely, the old owners had documented something so unique. The moldy papers left behind when I took over the junkyard might have had information, but those were long gone out of fear they'd make me sick. Still, I wouldn't give up that easily.

Searches of wolf bike, dog-head motorcycle, custom animal headlight, and more yielded results, just not the type I needed. Although, I did have a list of romance stories to check out, especially from Eve Langlais. She appeared rather prolific. And judging by her titles, perhaps a tad twisted.

I like twisted. I'd just spent more than twenty years living the most boring life ever. I wanted nothing more than to sink into an impossible fantasy, one that would make me feel alive.

After several hours of browsing, my head pounded, and my one good eye was ready to call it quits.

"I think it's time for bed, baby."

Blade eyed me, then the hallway to the laundry room and his doggy flap to the outside.

"Yes, I know you have to pee. I'll turn on the light." Poor baby. I wondered if he'd held it all night since I hadn't come home the previous evening.

As I waited in the laundry room for my cowardly dog to do his business, I got a load of laundry ready for the morning, including my cruddy jeans. I pulled the detective's card from my pocket. No official name on the front, just a generic OPP card with their main office address, a toll-free number, and an extension. On the back, written in ink, was a local number. Probably the detective's work cell. Rather than trash it, I tacked it onto my bulletin board that until now only held my pizza place flyer—because on Fridays, we always ordered in. Canadian extra cheese for me, and meat lovers for Blade.

Seeing the card had me thinking of the detective. Would he actually return to show me those mug shots? More likely, he'd demand that I come down to the station because I totally wanted to waste my time helping the cops solve a crime that would likely see the perps plea-dealing my assault down to probation and a promise to attend a substance abuse program. My city had been getting soft on crime ever since they'd decided that everyone was a victim. Someone beat the shit out of people for drug money? Not their fault. It was the addiction.

I was so tired of seeing the perps win. But what could I do?

My dog returned, scooting through that door flap as if the bogeyman nipped at his heels. For the first time ever, I slid the security flap down over the opening, sealing it shut. That night I didn't mind Blade's ginormous body squashing me as he huddled close for protection.

I hugged him, knowing no one would get into the house without him waking me up with his crying. And if that happened, the baseball bat by my bed would get a taste of blood. Although, it might be a good idea to pull a Negan from *The Walking Dead* and wrap some barbed wire around it for extra effect. To say that I remained rattled by the attack was an understatement.

I fully expected to have nightmares.

Instead, that night, I had the strangest dream...

CHAPTER 6

"WHAT ARE YOU DOING IN MY BED?"

The gruff voice startled me awake, only to realize that I slept still. Or was dead, seeing as how, when I sat up, I appeared to be a ghost outside my body—which still lay on the bed, eyes closed.

Freaky. Especially since Blade remained snoring atop my prone hump under the blanket.

Fingers snapped. "Earth to fucking stranger in my bed."

I swiveled my head to see a brute of a man standing near the door. Ever watch a show on bikers? Then you could easily picture six-feet-plus of bristling male wearing thigh-hugging jeans and a T-shirt, over which he'd layered an open leather jacket. The man had a square jaw and a salt-and-pepper bristle. Hair on top of his head? Unknown.

54

He could have been bald, considering he wore a dark blue bandanna. His scowl proved impressive.

"Who are you? The reaper?" I asked, trying not to freak out. "Am I dead?" Sure, he lacked a robe and a scythe, but he had the face of a person who wouldn't be swayed by threats or tears.

His brows rose. "You'd better not be dead. I don't need the cops banging on my door again."

The *again* didn't surprise. "Can you blame them? You look like the type who'd rob his own mother."

"What's that supposed to mean?" His ornery expression deepened. "I'll have you know I loved my mama and would have killed anyone who fucking did anything to her."

Only in my possible afterlife did I manage to insult the Grim Reaper. And then, to make things even better, I argued. "You need to leave. It's not my time to go yet." Death couldn't take me. I was too young to die.

I blamed the doctors and nurses at the hospital. They'd obviously missed something fatal. I glanced at my still-breathing body in bed. I jabbed a finger in his direction. "Aha, so long as my heart beats, you can't reap my soul. It's the rules!"

"Lady, you are acting crazy, and I am not in the mood. So, get your ass moving out the door so I can get some fucking sleep." The scowl punctuated his demand.

It didn't go over well. "Fuck you. I am not leaving. This is my house. Mine." I poked myself in the chest. "I bought it fair and square in an auction from the city."

"City don't own this place. I do. And I know for a fact I'm all paid up. I know better than to give those bureaucratic fuckers an excuse to come sniffing."

It hit me then who this must be. My overactive imagination had taken what Detective Walker had told me about the previous owner and the fact that he'd gone missing, and created a dream version. Apparently, I had classist and sexist views of the world, given I'd automatically made the previous owner a brutish male.

I laughed.

"What's so fucking funny?"

"After everything I've been through, I can't believe I'm arguing with a fake version of the previous owner." I rolled my eyes. "At least, I imagined you as hot." Really hot with his big body and how he oozed too much masculinity. Where the detective I'd lusted after today had the good looks of a preppy man, this guy had the kind of appearance that screamed: "Alpha male."

The bandanna got tugged, releasing a shaggy mass of dark hair threaded with silver. "Holy fuck, lady. I don't know what drugs you're on, but let's make one thing clear. I ain't touching you, so you can cry rape later."

I snorted. "Who says I want you to touch me, big man?" *It occurred to me that my dream had me fully healed. Both my eyes were open and working. Rising from the bed and trying to ignore my sleeping body, I didn't feel any aches or pains. It was only as I fully stood, and his gaze dropped to my body, that I recalled I'd gone to bed in only panties and a T-shirt that ended at my crotch.*

My turn to snap my fingers. "Eyes here, big boy," *I crooned.*

His gaze rose slowly, and his annoyance finally softened. "Maybe I should let you convince me to share my bed."

"My bed. My dream. My subconscious playing games. Blame the detective for telling me about the ghost."

"What detective? What have you been telling the cops?" *He loomed suddenly, putting me in his shadow. I was impressed by the realism. I could smell him. He reminded me of Irish Spring soap. He also smelled of exhaust, as if he'd just come off a motorcycle.*

"Worried about something?" I teased.

"You better not be telling lies to get me in trouble." His grip on my upper arms was firm, and when he yanked me on tiptoe so he could glare closely at me, our faces were inches apart. I got to see red flecks in his eyes.

"Aren't you a tough guy. Going to hit me next? Threaten to rape me?" I taunted him without fear. Don't get me wrong. My heart raced. My blood pounded through my veins, but with awareness. My dream might be a bit fucked up, but I didn't hate myself. I'd never let myself come to harm.

"I don't force women."

"Oh? Yet here you are, manhandling me."

The grip didn't loosen but raised me another half-inch—within striking distance of his mouth. "So what if I'm touching you? You're not made of glass. Do you need to be reminded you are in my house? Sleeping in my bed."

"Now you sound like Papa Bear."

"Stop trying to turn this into a joke," he grumbled.

"Fine, how about we turn this into a sex dream instead? Been a while since I had a good one." I used my free hands to grab his head and yank him down for a kiss. Caught his inhale of surprise before I firmly mashed my mouth to his. Amazing how I *could feel him. For a few seconds at least, before he thrust me from him, barking, "Why do I hear a dog?"*

"Woof. Woof." I blinked awake to find Blade standing on my bed, barking at the doorway to my bedroom. Instantly, I rolled and grabbed my baseball bat, ready to swing into action.

Only no one was there.

The moment I realized it, my dog did, too. With a mighty yawn, Blade lay down and went back to sleep.

As for me?

I pressed my fingers to lips that still tingled and wondered for a second if I'd just kissed Detective Walker's ghost.

CHAPTER 7

IT TOOK ME A WHILE TO FALL BACK ASLEEP. WHEN I did eventually wake, I found myself in a full-on sweat. Not the menopause kind but rather my heating-blanket-of-a-dog kind.

"Get off me," I grumbled, giving Blade a shove. He rolled over to his side of the bed—which was three-quarters of it compared to my sliver on the edge—and the furball went back to sleep under the comforter I'd kicked off.

Good morning to me. I ached all over. My body made sure I knew about every single bruise. More than I recalled having the day before. It also served as a reminder that crouching and bending over a motor for more than twelve hours didn't agree with my forties body. I'd need a gallon of coffee, some Tylenol,

Advil, and, hell, maybe even an aspirin. Then, I'd be good to go.

Once I managed to get out of bed.

It happened, eventually, with much groaning. Apparently, enough that my dog opened an eye to check on me. Saw I lived and went back to snoring.

My lips twisted. "I'm fine. Thanks for caring." I shuffled to the bathroom, a thing of pink, black, and white tile that hadn't been updated—ever. Honestly, I didn't see the point as the damned shit had no cracks, and with a bit of grout cleaner, looked good as new. I just ignored the hideous color scheme and pretended I loved living in a retro paradise. Made me wonder about the previous owner and why he'd kept it intact.

A peek in the mirror over the sink showed me looking like something out of an abused women's pamphlet. Purple cheekbone, the radiating bruise extending outward in green and yellow as well as wrapping around my eye. But in good news, the swelling had gone down enough that I could open it a slit. Not recommended, however, given it immediately teared. Maybe I should get myself an eye patch. Then I could have a cool junkyard nickname like One-Eyed Allie. Or That Pirate Bitch.

Making light didn't take away from the fact that I wouldn't be winning any beauty pageants today. In positive news, I could pee without any pain and, yay, no blood! Praise be, I had escaped any internal injuries.

Over my breakfast of Alphabets and orange juice, while Blade scarfed down his bowl of the same, albeit minus the milk, I resumed my internet searching but this time looked up the junkyard I'd bought. The worn-out sign I'd repainted used to say *Steel Deals*—which someone had crossed out and graffitied with *Suck Dick*. I'd painted the whole thing black and then, in a bluish-white, stenciled *Bits and Bolts*, which was my play on *Bits and Bites*, a snack I loved in the cheddar cheese flavor. So salty.

Mmm. I should really pick up a bag. Only one, because I would likely inhale the entire package in one sitting. Okay, maybe not inhale. I'd suck the flavor from each piece before crunching it to bits. The numb tongue the next day? Totally worth it.

Anyhow, back to my search. *Steel Deals* was apparently a popular combination on the internet. Only six hundred and fifty-five million search results.

After page five, I knew I'd have to go at it a different way. I popped in the address for the junkyard. First thing I got was a map—because that really helped.

Then a mention of the property auction with very few details other than that it was commercially zoned property with an attached residence. The writeup included the structures on the property, and the notes mentioned the metal scrap yard aspect. All shit I knew, and the reason I'd chosen to bid. I might not be some super climate activist, but I did like the idea of helping recycle metal parts.

Maybe I should take that welding course offered at Algonquin College. I could do quite a bit myself, but I'd love to learn the finer techniques. I could buy myself a Mig welder for the shop. Offer to do custom metalwork. Make some art with the unused parts in my yard.

Focus! I was getting distracted. I ate more soggy cereal as I kept flipping pages on my tablet, perusing all kinds of searches that did nothing to advance my knowledge. There had to be a better way of finding what I wanted.

The detective had said something about the original owner having gone missing.

My bowl pushed aside, I leaned forward, only to tilt my face sideways at a slurping noise. My dog, realizing he'd gotten caught licking my bowl, sucked his tongue back in. "Nice try. I saw that."

He offered me a *Who me?* tilt of his head. Is it weird I said it in Scooby-Doo's voice? For some reason, the one made me think of the other. My dog was just as cowardly. As for me, I'd yet to decide who I was. One thing was for sure, I lacked the Velma gene. But, apparently, had a lucky one because I caught my break on page seventeen. Almost missed it skimming.

An archived newspaper article had the words *junkyard* and *murder* highlighted. It took forever for the archived story to load, and I got the gist—salacious undertones and all. The basics consisted of one Killian Mahoney, owner of Steel Deals, being questioned about the sudden surge in possibly gang-related murders in Ottawa. As to why Killian Mahoney, aka Junkdog, came to the cops' notice? He'd once belonged to a since-disbanded gang from Toronto known as the Trikillz who liked to eliminate their rivals by gutting their victims, though not with a knife. Instead, they apparently wore gloves fitted with three long blades that sliced like claws. Very distinctive.

Back to the mounting murders in Ottawa. Guess what trait the bodies all shared? And what a coincidence that the only Trikillz member not behind bars lived in the area. There was also conjecture that the junkyard had been a front for drugs and illegal guns.

They believed that when the cops got too close, Mahoney bolted. He was never seen or heard from again. And the murders stopped.

The comment section proved even more interesting than the article.

Cops should have left him alone. He was cleaning up the scum in town.

Someone needs to put out the Junkdog's beacon so he knows he's needed. Which I figured meant the equivalent of a Bat-Signal.

Thanks for ruining a good thing.

The gist being that the people's deaths had left the world a better place. Cold. Harsh. Probably true, though. Some people were a waste of space and air.

The article didn't have a picture of Mahoney, only the junkyard sign and fence. Suddenly, I had to know what Killian Mahoney looked like. I typed in his name, got bunches of people on social media, though none of them a late-forties-something man. But I persevered, and with a combination of his name and the gang he used to belong to, located a picture. Taken by someone as he emerged from the police station wearing a scowl, a leather jacket, a dark T-shirt, and jeans.

My jaw hit the floor hard.

It's him.

The man in my dreams.

CHAPTER 8

THE SHOCK HIT ME HARD. HOW COULD I HAVE dreamed of Killian Mahoney, a guy I'd never met? I'd have sworn I'd never seen him before, and yet there he was, on my computer screen, looking exactly as he had in my dream.

Or had I met his ghost?

"That's just crazy," I muttered. I'd never believed in the supernatural. Blame the detective for putting the idea in my head. A dead man hadn't visited me last night. Blame all the pills I'd popped for the pain. As to how I knew exactly what he looked like, down to the way his hair waved back from his face? I must have come across a picture of him and just forgotten.

Right?

"Right," I said aloud, and I could have

sworn cold fingers trailed over my skin. Goose-bumps erupted, and I stood so fast from my chair, it wobbled. No one there. Of course, there wasn't. My house didn't have a poltergeist.

I slammed my laptop lid shut, which startled my dog, who bolted as if a ghost chased him. A ghost required a dead person. No one claimed that Mahoney had died. The detective had implied he'd run off. What if he'd never been seen again because someone had killed him and buried the body? I couldn't think of a better place than a junkyard to do it.

I glanced out my kitchen window. *I'd better not find any dead bodies.* It would probably put a cramp in my rebuild schedule for the Plymouth.

Thinking of which, I should get going on it. "You coming?" I asked my cowardly dog, knowing he probably hid on the other side of the couch.

Blade peeked. I could see his Scooby eyes asking, *"Is it safe?"*

"I'll protect you, baby. Come on. Let's get a move on, and remember, don't poop on the path." Because I'd be pissed if I stepped in it.

Bad enough, I had to clean giant piles of shit, scrubbing it from my boots sucked.

Blade's bushy tail wagged. He would totally shit somewhere I could admire. I could almost smell it already.

Sigh.

"After you." I swung open the side door, and Blade took a step outside, stopped, looked around suspiciously, then eyed me with a lolling tongue.

"My big, brave guard dog," I praised, patting his head as I walked by.

He remained at my side as we took the path to the junkyard. I thought about opening the main gates, but that would require me walking all the way over and then back. My sore body protested that kind of exertion. I should see if I could find myself an ATV or golf cart for scooting around in. Use some tires to pad corners and make the yard into a track for fun.

Totally crazy at my age. Whatever. I still wanted to do it.

Until I had some zippy wheels, though, I would walk my lazy ass over to that gate and open it for potential buyers. Because, hello, I was trying to be a businesswoman, which meant I needed clients. Even if they weren't as fun as playing with the Plymouth.

Or the mystery bike.

I couldn't stop thinking about it. Wondering what it used to look like in its day. How would it purr once I got that motor going? I really wanted to find out.

The new padlock I'd installed came undone easily enough with my key, and the gates creaked as I pulled them open for business. I pasted a sign on my office door—*In the garage. Knock first*—so I didn't wiz my pants in fear.

With the note in place, I headed for my real office, proud of myself for being a responsible junkyard owner while doing something I loved. Multi-tasking at its best.

Blade followed me into the garage and went right to the chair I'd dragged into the corner. His chair. It held some of the toys he babied.

Funny how everything scared my dog except for the power tools when I worked. I could do all kinds of hammering, drilling, sawing, you name it, and Blade snored away.

Usually, he did. Today, he watched the bike. I understood the fascination. Ignoring the Plymouth, I couldn't help but stroke my fingers over the wolf's nose. The metalwork gave me a thrill, a zing that electrified. For a moment, I could have sworn the headlight holes sparked red.

My dog growled.

I blinked, and the worn bike stared back, the lenses of the lights filthy with grime and probably no longer any good.

A glance at Blade showed him glaring at the motorcycle.

"It's okay, baby. It might look like a big, mean wolf, but by the time I'm done fixing it, it will be the sleekest of cats."

The bike shifted away from me, and I reached quickly to steady it.

"Wobbly sucker. Guess I should invest in a proper stand so you don't land on me when I start working on you." I could hardly wait. I'd only ever worked on one bike, and that was in my teens. Still, two wheels or four, the concept remained the same.

Given the Plymouth still had a few more days of work before it went to get painted, I grabbed a notepad and a pencil—chewed...by me, I should add—before gnawing on the end. It helped me think. I jotted notes, items I'd need for the rebuild, tools to gather. I had most of them, although I might need to check my Allen key situation. I vaguely recalled bikes using some strange sizes.

Intent on my task, the knocking at the door startled me, and I almost fell off my stool.

My lazy dog kept staring at the bike, not even looking in the direction of the possible intruder.

I tucked the pencil behind my ear as I grumbled, "Maybe I should get a cat."

The insult didn't do a thing to motivate my dog.

I made sure to grip a wrench before yelling, "Who is it?"

"Detective Walker." He stuck his head in and gifted me the Colgate-straight-and-white smile of a man who'd never missed a dental appointment. I shouldn't talk. I didn't either. "Is this a bad time?"

Petty me wanted to say it was never a good time to talk to the po-po; however, he had shown up, which I could admit surprised me. I wouldn't have thought a case of tweakers getting rough merited an actual detective paying me a personal visit.

"Sure, come on in." I tucked away my

notepad and scooted my stool in the direction of the car as Walker entered.

A low whistle emerged from him. "Nice. That's a Plymouth Fury, right?"

I nodded. "Surprised you recognize it. Most people mistake it for a Belvedere."

"As if I wouldn't recognize Christine." He ran his hand over the smooth hood. "You going to paint it red like the books and movie?"

"I don't know. I thought about it, but it seems kind of too obvious." I wrinkled my nose.

"At the same time, any other color might prove distracting."

"Yeah." Red would garner attention and probably the higher price.

"What's that hunk of junk?" He pointed at the bike leaning on the workbench.

"A trashed bike. Found it where I was attacked." I didn't mention that it would be my next project.

"Should have left it there." His lips turned down in disapproval.

"You kidding? I couldn't leave it there. This hunk of metal saved me." I patted the dented fender. "It's going to be beautiful once I clean it up."

"Are you sure you want to do that considering who owned it?"

The remark stunned me into momentary silence before I sputtered, "You recognize the bike?"

"Yeah. It used to belong to the guy who owned the junkyard way back when."

Having done my homework, I muttered, "Killian 'Junkdog' Mahoney."

The detective's face tightened. "I see you've heard of him."

"Not really. Mostly read that he was the previous owner of the yard and disappeared when the cops started harassing him."

"We had reason. Mahoney was not an upstanding citizen."

The use of *we* prompted me to ask, "Did you have many run-ins with him?"

"Yeah. But the guy was slick. Never could pin anything on him." He sounded disappointed.

"I found a newspaper article that hinted he might have been involved in some grisly murders."

"Not just might. Mahoney was our main

suspect. We'd applied for a warrant to arrest him; only someone ratted us out. By the time we went to serve it, he'd split."

My curiosity wanted to know. "Did anyone search for him?"

"Yes. To no avail. He remains a wanted man to this day."

"For a wanted man, I had the hardest time finding anything about him online."

"Would you like me to send you his official poster? I believe they're still offering a reward."

"Yes, actually. A picture would be useful," was my pert reply.

"Useful for what?"

"What if he comes back here?"

The detective blinked at me. "Why would he do that?"

"Because, duh, this used to belong to him."

"Not anymore."

"But would he recognize that?" I couldn't help thinking of dream-version Mahoney, accusing me of sleeping in his bed.

"He's not coming back."

"If you say," I said with as much singsong doubt as I could manage. "I don't suppose your department has an updated sketch of what he might look like since it's been more than ten years?"

"No, and I doubt you have anything to worry about. Guy like him, the type of lifestyle he indulged in, it's doubtful he's still alive."

"But he could be," I insisted.

"Do you have something to tell me?" His gaze pierced me. "Did you see something? Someone?"

"Still wondering if I see ghosts?" I smirked. "Ain't nothing spooky around here, Detective."

"I'd disagree. Or are you saying you're no longer worried about those men who attacked you? We've yet to find them."

Zing. The reminder hit me in the gut. I sat down hard on my stool and sent it rolling with a kick of my heels.

"Ms. Collins? Allie?" He crouched and showed concern without touching.

"Fine, just jarred. I've been trying to pretend it didn't happen."

"That might not be wise."

"Says you. Forgetting it sounds just right to me. After all, what are the chances it will happen again? One in a million?" Left unsaid: Even once more would be too much.

"I'd say there's a high probability they'll come back."

My jaw dropped. "Well, that's not re-assuring."

"It's the truth. Because you had money on-site, they'll remember this place."

I wagged a finger as the solution hit me. "I'll stop keeping cash in my office."

"How are you going to let them know?"

Good point. "What do you suggest?"

He eyed my dog. "I don't suppose it actu-ally moves if it thinks you're in danger."

Blade had chosen to sleep as I conversed with the po-po. Not exactly good backup.

"My dog is more likely to pee on someone in fear than bite them."

"Then you should think about adding some security."

"Sounds expensive. Personally, I was going to whack them with this wrench." I hefted it and smacked it against my palm.

He snorted. "How well did fighting them off work last time?"

Another verbal slap. "They took me by surprise."

"And will do so again if you don't take steps to prevent it."

"What are you suggesting? I can't afford a security guard, and if you say sell the business and move, I'm going to tell you where to shove that idea."

"Statistically, rural areas are safer for women so long as you're not in an abusive domestic situation. I would suggest, however, getting a weapon you can wield that will do more damage."

I arched a brow. "Why, officer, are you encouraging me to invest in a firearm for defense?"

"I didn't say buy a gun." A disparaging tone showed his lack of amusement. "But you could get yourself an electrified cattle prod."

Surprise kept me silent for a second before I sputtered, "Isn't that illegal?"

"Only if you tell the authorities it's to use against people."

"I don't have any cows, though."

"If anyone asks, tell them you have a coyote problem."

I tilted my head. "Sounds like you're suggesting I skirt the law."

"Don't know what you're talking about." He offered an enigmatic smile and a wink.

Sexy bastard. And his suggestion was not

that bad. Things would have gone differently that night if I'd been able to shock my assailants. I wondered if a certain giant online merchant would deliver any with free one-day shipping. If not, then surely a livestock store would have some.

"So, was this visit simply to point out my inadequate security? Or did you have another reason, Detective?"

"As promised, I brought some pictures for you to browse. Shall we see if you recognize any of your assailants?"

I hadn't noticed the tablet in his hand until he offered it to me. A simple, generic brand tucked into a fake leather sleeve. It went from sleep mode right into a gallery of mug shots.

"There are several pages. Swipe left or right, depending on if you're going forward or back."

"Bring on the fun." As I dragged my finger to flip, I shook my head. "Nope. Nope. Nope." The faces I swept by mostly wore grim expressions, except for the guy with the loony grin and crazy eyes.

As I kept rejecting images, the detective wandered to stand over the bike. His body was tense as if he expected the hunk of metal to attack him.

I got to the end of the images and exclaimed, "Done."

"And?"

"None of them look familiar."

"You're sure?" The detective whirled, and he must have caught the bike because it shifted and fell against him.

Rather than catch the falling metal and lean it back against the workbench, he violently shoved it from him as if it were contagious.

I almost laughed. "Afraid you'll get dirty?" A legitimate fear, given the filth coating it. Motor oil did not come out of fabric without a credit card to buy a replacement.

"More like startled." He offered a rueful smile. "And also not a bike guy. I like a roof over my head when it rains."

"I totally get it. Me, I used to love riding."

"Used to?" he prodded.

"I haven't ridden in more than twenty years. I'll admit, I miss that vibration and power between my legs." Said in the most salacious fashion possible.

The detective didn't miss a beat as he replied, "Is that an invitation?"

Surprised, I gaped as he added, "Given the mug shots were a bust, I'll let you get back to work. Call me if you think of anything. Although, I expect we'll see each other again shortly."

We would? Before I could say a word, he left, and I smiled.

I might look like I went a few rounds with Tyson, but a cute guy who I pegged to be about my age had flirted. My ego could use the stroking, as could other parts of me, so I really hoped he came back. Maybe with a bottle of wine and a love of frozen dinners.

The bike had landed at an angle. I righted it before I straddled the frame. How would it feel once I got the motor running? The grumbling power between my legs.

A jolt hit me through the crotch, which made little sense. I frowned as I glanced down.

Forget the motor. Maybe I'd start with the electrical.

CHAPTER 9

THE NEXT FEW DAYS PASSED NORMALLY.

My bruises faded, my anxiety lessened, and my dog made the brave and bold move of woofing when the sweetest old lady insisted on dropping off her departed husband's car along with a wad of cash if I'd agree to let her hit it a few times.

"You don't have to pay me. I'll take the car. It's in decent condition."

Mrs. Macpherson shook her head. "It won't be after I'm done with it. I wanted to get it out of the way before I went at it."

"May I ask why?"

"Bertram loved that damned car more than me." Said in the cutest, little-old-lady voice.

How much damage could she do to the very clean Oldsmobile?

Apparently, she carried much pent-up rage. About the only thing she didn't dent was the motor. Even the tires didn't survive.

However, the widow beamed, and my dog wagged his tail as tiny-but-fierce Mrs. Macpherson pulled out a dog cookie from her massive purse. "Have a great day, dear."

I'd rather have interesting nights. Ever since my attack, I was tucked into my house, doors and windows locked, well before dark, watching the boob tube.

Boring. Also an indication of just how badly those fuckers had scared me. I was missing out on hours that I could be working. Or, as I sometimes liked to call it, relaxing. Because my anxiety only eased when I kept busy.

By Friday of that week, the Plymouth was done, and Danny took it using a flatbed tow truck. He promised to have it painted within two weeks. With my shop empty, I was finally free for my next project.

The wolf bike. It took center position, sitting on the lift I'd splurged on to ensure that it wouldn't fall again. I'd not touched it since I'd made that list of parts and ordered them. I'd known that once I got started, I'd get sucked in, and the Plymouth wouldn't get finished. Now, though, it was mine to play with.

The jolt didn't surprise me as much this time when I ran my fingers over the frame. I'd come to expect the electrical tingle every time I touched it. Soon, I'd pinpoint the culprit and fix it.

I started taking the bike apart, laying the pieces on a tarp in the order I removed them. A trick my dad had taught me. Once I had all the parts removed, I would clean them one by one and check for damage, replacing anything I couldn't fix.

A sudden knock startled me, and I nicked my finger on the bracket for the muffler, tearing skin enough that I bled.

"Fuck." I popped the cut flesh into my mouth but not before my blood smeared the bike.

The detective stuck his head in. "Is this a bad time?"

I shook my head and stood, removing my finger from my mouth—which, in retrospect, I should have washed first given the dirt and oil. "Nope, we're good. What's up?" I wasn't one hundred percent bruise-free, but I no longer needed an eyepatch, and if one ignored the yellowing on half my face, I looked mostly normal.

"I was in the area and thought I'd check on you."

"No news on my case, I take it?"

He shook his head. "I am keeping an ear open for any other similar attacks."

"I did as you said and invested in some motion-sensor cameras." Which, somehow, had missed the detective's arrival. Fucking technology only worked when it wanted to.

"That's a good start. Did you get something to defend yourself?"

"I did. I got the prod and some pepper spray."

"Good, although it would be better if you never had to use them."

"No shit."

He eyed the bike. "I see you're determined to fix that hunk of junk."

"It will fetch me a tidy bundle once I'm done with it."

"Speaking of bundle." He held out a pair of tickets. "Someone at work was giving these away. Some kind of dinner theatre combo. Interested in going?"

I could have pointed out the impropriety of a detective on my case asking me out. Then I looked at his hopeful dimple, the width of his shoulders in his suit jacket, and the fact that he looked really good with that day-old scruff shading his jawline.

"Can I grab a quick shower first?"

In the end, I got two hours to get ready as he left and returned later to pick me up. A good thing I had plenty of time because the shower and cleaning out the grease from under my nails wasn't the longest part. Choosing an outfit proved most difficult. I'd not dated since my divorce. Add in the twenty-some years of marriage to The Jerk, and I was woefully unprepared.

Dress? Pants? Casual? Fancy? Would he expect me to put out? Did I want to have sex? Because a yes meant matching bra and underwear, also some trimming of my private bits so he didn't scream at the massive Venus bush growing down there. A dress, and a possibility of sex, meant shaving the pits and legs, too. So much work.

It should be noted, the few times I'd randomly hooked up with guys, I didn't give a shit. One-night stands didn't merit much preparation as it was about sexual release and nothing else. In the case of the detective, he gave me tingles, the kind that wanted maybe more than just one date.

Did women my age have boyfriends? Wait, the correct term now was partner. Whatever. I needed to stop freaking. He'd asked me out. No big deal. I should go. Enjoy myself and see what happened.

Could be nothing. Maybe the chemistry was one-sided.

Then why ask me to go?

Funny how the prospect of a guy liking me took away from my confidence and put me back in the anxious body of a teenager with her does-he-like-me-or-not mentality.

The bruising had diminished enough that it could be hidden by makeup. For once, my long hair cooperated with my blow-dryer to take on a silken sheen. I settled on my little black dress, which wrapped around me and had been used for everything in the last five years from funerals to a friend's daughter getting married. I'd livened it up with a blue scarf and shoes. Don't judge. The choices in my closet proved limited.

There was the floral summer dress that fit

me shapelessly and The Jerk used to call *the muumuu*. Well, sorry, but I wasn't into the tiny, strapless, mid-thigh numbers his young chippie liked to sport. I wasn't about to slip on my ice princess dress which I'd bought for Halloween years ago and never dared to wear.

Going through my closet also showed a lack of almost anything without a grease stain. I really needed to start separating my work stuff from my going-out stuff. Once I got going-out stuff.

I did a little better with shoes. I found those easy to buy and, with mixing and matching, could turn my little black dress into something trendy and...

Nope. I needed to stop making excuses for my lazy wardrobe. Tomorrow, I'd online shop, because fuck wasting time heading into the city and going store to store.

For makeup, I had mascara and eyeliner. Did Chapstick count as lipstick?

The final product wasn't half-bad. Although, my hair could apparently use a cut. It had been a while since it'd seen scissors, but at least I could claim the color as mine. I might have hit my late forties, but like my mother and her mother before her, I'd so far missed the grays. Except for the one in my pubes, which died a plucked death. Gray hair down there? Just wrong.

I opted for matching undergarments; the red lace underwear stiff from never having been worn. The lace bra, with its very full cups, made my tits into a shelf of art. Since I wanted to be sexy, I skipped the lacy camisole and let my cleavage hang out of the dress—the swell of them revealed by the slit in the wrap-around fabric framed by a hint of the crimson brassiere.

Too much? Guess I'd soon find out. I just hoped it didn't come across as desperate. Walking meant being very aware of the thin wedge of lace between my thighs. Would anyone know I'd worn my get-lucky underpants? Bad enough that I knew. It caused my cheeks to heat, but also my pussy because I felt sexy and *hawt*.

Ready, I headed back to the living room and my moping dog. He lay on the couch, head on his paws, watching me with the biggest eyes. My fault. I'd given him his rawhide before going for my shower, worried I'd forget.

From experience, Blade understood that him getting a rawhide meant I would be leaving.

Blade hated being alone. He would go after my boots if I didn't give him something to chew. I'd broken those suckers in with blisters and hisses of pain. No way did I want to work in a new pair.

"You be a good boy while I'm gone," I reminded as I debated on a coat. Nothing I owned worked with the dress. A going-out coat—another thing for the list of things I should buy. Going through more money. At this rate, I might actually have to actively work to ensure a steady income.

"Have you gone pee?" I'd been leaving his doggy door locked since the attack, too nervous at the thought of one of those bastards squeezing through and maybe surprising me while I slept.

Blade uttered a long-suffering sigh at my question, but he knew the drill. He lumbered from the couch, and I followed him to the doggy door, which I unsealed. I watched from the window as he slowly found a spot to do his business.

Poor Blade. Hopefully, I'd either get over my fear soon, or they'd catch those assholes.

With him good for the night, we headed back into the living room to wait. I'd see the detective's lights before he arrived, which had me thinking. What should I call him? Detective? Mister Walker? Did I ever get his first name?"

The question got answered when he knocked on the door, having pulled in behind my car, a very boring Ford sedan that I could count on in any kind of weather.

I opened and, despite expecting him, found myself flustered. "Hi, Detective. I mean Mr. Walker." I wanted to bite my tongue to shut up as I finished with a high-pitched, "How nice to see you."

He winced and immediately chuckled. "I guess I should have told you before, call me Brayden."

"And I'm Alyssa, Allie, actually, to my friends." I waved a hand. "And that lazy butt over there, pretending to be a dog, is Blade." I prattled, then almost slapped myself because... hello, he knew all that.

Brayden eyed my pup and drawled, "I'm going to guess you didn't name him."

"No. If I had, he'd probably have some kind of weird car name."

"My last cat was called Fluffs."

The admission startled. "You're a cat person?"

"My ex was. But when we split, I kept the feline."

"How long were you together?" I could have slapped myself a second after I asked.

But he didn't seem bothered. "Me and the ex? Three years. The cat? Almost fifteen before cancer took her."

"I'm recently divorced after twenty some years of marriage." A blurted admission.

"Kids?"

I shook my head and then made the shocking admission. "Never wanted any." A nod from Brayden rather than condemnation. "You?" I asked.

"I thought about it. However, I enjoy my life, the freedom to go and do as I please."

"Within the boundaries of the law," I quipped.

"Not always," he murmured before saying, "Shall we go?"

My dog didn't start howling until I locked the door.

Brayden eyed the house. "Is he going to be okay?"

"Yeah. He has separation issues. If it gets

bad, he'll cuddle his pillow." Wrapped in my T-shirt of the day.

"Maybe next time we'll watch a movie on the couch so he doesn't have to worry." Casually said and implying that this wasn't a one-time thing. That would depend on how good he turned out to be tonight.

The detective's company proved nice. He held courteous, old-school views on women, which meant doors being opened, chairs being pulled out, and him respecting me when I said no to wine with dinner.

First dates should always be mostly sober, or so some lady on that video social networking service claimed—something about not having second-date regret when you eventually spent time with them without the haze of alcohol.

Brayden stuck to lemon water and coffee with dessert. I ignored the dating advice about not ordering anything and flirtatiously asking for a bite of his. Fuck that. I wanted my own piece of cake—chocolate with whipped cream and cherries. I groaned as I ate it.

He'd ordered the pie, which smelled and looked good, but he barely touched his wedge. Maybe I'd scam a piece when I was done.

We sat side by side at a two-person table, facing a stage featuring some play I couldn't have described. I'd been having too much fun talking with the dry-witted detective.

"Can I have a bite?" he asked, his hand lightly coming to rest on my thigh.

"My cake. Eat your own dessert." I jabbed my fork at it.

"But yours looks much yummier." His gaze lingered on my mouth.

I tingled between the legs and leaned close enough to whisper, "It's delicious."

"Mmm, I've no doubt. Let me taste." He rubbed his mouth on mine.

A phone buzzed.

His phone. He grimaced. "Work. Can I have a second?"

"Sure, take as long as you need." He left, and I hit the ladies' room before returning for the end of the play with no idea why there was so much laughter. I sipped my cold coffee and thought: His place or mine?

The date was going that well. He had the hots for me, that much was clear. I was ready to drop my panties for him. I could see this ending in bed.

He returned as people began rising from their seats, preparing to leave.

"Sorry. I didn't mean for that to take so long."

"It's fine."

He helped me from my seat, standing closer than needed, staring down at me. "Did you want to go somewhere else? A coffee shop, perhaps? I know a place that does milkshakes."

As he sought reasons to extend the date, I said, "I've got coffee at my place."

His lips curved. "That sounds fantastic."

His fingers wrapped around mine as we headed out, following the jostling stream of other guests. When someone bumped me in passing, he drew me close to his body and tucked us out of the way into an alley.

"Let's wait for the crush to die down." He stared down at me, and his knuckles brushed my cheek.

Such a gentleman. I dragged his head down. "I know what we can do while we wait."

He only hesitated a fraction of a second before meeting my kiss with pure, fiery passion.

His fingers laced behind my head, threading into my hair. My back pressed against the building wall. My leg straddled the outside of his, his hard thigh between mine where I wantonly rode it.

If we kept this up, I'd come. In an alley. I whispered, "We should go back to my place."

Brayden drove fast, his hand on my leg, my dress hem pushed up so he palmed flesh. I pulsed wetly and wished he'd move it up a little higher.

The whole ride to my place acted as foreplay. I was ready to pounce by the time he pulled into my driveway.

The moment Brayden helped me out of the car, he had me pushed against it, kissing me, groping me. We might have ended up doing it right there, only his phone pinged.

He groaned. "Not now."

"Ignore it," I whispered, biting his lower lip.

It dinged again, and he sighed. "I'd better check on that." A single glance at the screen turned his smoldering expression into a grimace. "I'm afraid I need to beg a raincheck. Work needs me."

"Can you be a few minutes late?" I purred.

He looked pained as my hand slid up his thigh. "I would like nothing more than to finish what we started, but I also won't rush our first time. Can I come by to see you tomorrow?" He cupped my ass and growled the request against my lips.

"You'd better, or I'll be taking care of what you started myself." I still might once he left.

"That's just plain cruel." He kissed me, and I felt his reluctance as he pulled away. "Tomorrow. I'll bring dinner so we don't have to go anywhere."

"Sounds good." A smiling and horny me entered the house. The date had gone better than expected. Even my lug of a dog peeing on my foot in happiness that I'd survived the dark and returned home couldn't ruin it.

I went to bed thinking of my date.

And dreamed of another man.

CHAPTER 10

KILLIAN MAHONEY GLARED AT ME. GHOST OR dream apparition, he still appeared mighty impressive as he snarled, "What were you doing in my garage?"

"*Your* garage?" I snorted. "It's mine because you're not real." A firm claim despite my subconscious apparently worrying that he might exist. Did I fear Mahoney coming back to take the junkyard from me? Legally, he didn't have a leg to stand on and would be arrested if he tried.

"You're the one who's unreal. Who gave you permission to mess with my stuff? I saw you touching my bike." His brows tugged together in a mighty frown.

That didn't scare me. "It's my stuff now. I bought it all, fair and square."

"Like fuck, you did. This place and everything in it belongs to me. And, right now, that includes you." He growled menacingly.

"You did not just try to claim me as property," I huffed. I went toe-to-toe with the tall Mahoney and glared up at his chiseled chin. I poked him in the solid chest. Definitely a dream because ghosts didn't have bodies. "I am not a woman who's going to let a man treat her like she's worthless. You're the worthless one. You left and didn't pay your bills. Now, the junkyard is mine. Legally. And even if you *did* exist and came back, you wouldn't be able to sue me for it 'cause the cops are still looking to arrest you for murder."

"Fucking cops. They had no case 'cause I didn't do it."

"As if you'd admit it," I scoffed. "The evidence is pretty convincing."

"Evidence of what?" he riposted.

"You going to deny that your old gang used to like slicing people into ribbons?"

"They did. I didn't. Although, being associated with those who did, landed me in the hospital with multiple gunshot wounds. I cleaned up my act when they released me from rehab."

"Did you? Or were you good at pretending?" I fired a counterargument. "The cops wouldn't arrest you without evidence."

"Then you're obviously not well acquainted with the law. They'll do anything to declare a case closed."

"Let me guess, next you'll claim they were framing you."

"Wouldn't surprise me. The detective on the case hated me."

"I'm sure he had a reason. Perhaps your obnoxious personality, for starters."

That got Mahoney glaring. "Fuck if I know why he kept coming around, harassing me."

"Because you were a killer."

"Don't you think if I was a killer, I would have taken care of him?"

"A smart murderer wouldn't kill the cop suspicious of him."

"How about a guy who didn't murder anyone and didn't have a way to convince said cop of his innocence?"

I rolled my eyes. "It doesn't really matter anymore. You disappeared. The junkyard went to auction for unpaid taxes. I bought it, fair and square. So, I have nothing to feel guilty about. You're just a figment of my imagination anyway." I waited for him to disappear as I confronted my conscience.

Mahoney continued glowering. "Fuck you, I disappeared. I would never leave the Ottawa Valley area."

"Facts say otherwise."

"I wouldn't," he insisted, pacing in my dream. "Not without my sister, and I'd have needed the money from selling the junkyard to take care of her properly elsewhere."

Well, that took an unexpected twist. "What sister?"

"My baby sister. Ginny. She was born with Down syndrome. Since she couldn't take care of herself when my folks died, I had her placed in an assisted care place in West End Ottawa."

"I don't know anything about your sister." But I did love how my brain was trying to make his story more interesting. "If you didn't leave, then what happened to you?"

He glanced down at his body. "Nothing. I'm right here. This dream makes no sense."

I outright laughed. "This is my dream, not yours. Nice try, though." Then, on a lark, I asked, "What year do you think it is?"

"What kind of dumb question is that?"

"The kind that you're going to avoid because my dream version of you doesn't have an answer." I snorted. "This is so weird. I don't know why I'm even thinking about you. We've never met. Never will."

"What are you talking about? This is the second time I've found you on my property. And as I recall, didn't *you* kiss *me*?"

"You can remember that but not where you went after you disappeared?"

"You're the only one claiming I disappeared." He remained close to me.

"Because it's the truth."

"Perhaps I need something to jar my memories."

"Like what?"

"I'm thinking another kiss."

"How is a kiss supposed to help? I'm not a part of your past."

"No, but you seem tied to my present and future." He whispered it against my lips as he bent to put them within range.

"I'm kind of seeing someone," I huffed hotly, yet I didn't move away.

"Have you fucked?" Hard emphasis on the consonant.

"Not yet." And only because he'd gotten a cock-blocking call.

"Then you're fair game," he said before taking my lips.

And I mean he *took* them.

Lavished them with attention. Caressed and tugged, his tongue slipping and sliding. I ignited with desire and rubbed wantonly against him. Things might have gotten naked and quick if my phone hadn't gone off, startling me awake.

As I lay there, wide-eyed and panting, my phone beeped again. A glance to the side showed an alert. Motion detected.

Someone was in the junkyard!

CHAPTER 11

THE NUMBER ONE THING TO DO WHEN YOUR cameras tell you there is an intruder? Check the video. Because, at this point, I'd had several false alarms. Who knew I had so many raccoons using my yard as a shortcut? Skunks, too. The way my heart pounded, you'd have thought it predetermined that my alert would be more than just vermin.

The grainy black-and-white video had the night vision lens recording. It caught motion, a slide of shadow across the screen, big enough to be a person. There one second, gone the next. I checked the office camera. No alerts. Flipping it to live mode didn't show anyone there. A glance through the app for more warnings came up empty.

Only the single camera had caught anything.

The tip of my thumb met the gnawing flat edge of my teeth. Did I have enough to call the police? Even I wondered about what I'd seen. Perhaps it was simply a shadow with no actual person behind it.

I glanced at the clock. Three a.m. I could still get back to bed. I usually didn't rise until at least six.

No point in bothering. I'd just toss and turn, awake, wondering if someone was in the junkyard. Sneaking up on my house. Making a fool of me again. Scaring me...

Some people reacted with terror by becoming even more scared. Me? I found myself getting pissed. How dare someone think it was okay to trespass on my property?

I wouldn't be a victim. Not anymore. I armed myself with the taser rod. Not exactly a cattle prod, but it'd only cost me a hundred bucks. Turned out you could purchase anything online, even supposedly illegal stuff. Like my pepper spray. I'd gotten the super-burny, Cajun spice kind—or so the dude who'd dropped it off had claimed. He'd also said that he'd used it to season pork before barbecuing it. Personally, I'd hold off trying it on any meat hitting my lips.

My dog stayed in my bed, head under the covers. Poor thing, so terrified.

"I'll protect you, baby." I'd protect us both.

I had my phone tucked in my front pocket. I could still call 9-1-1 if it turned out to be an emergency. I didn't want to be the hysterical lady who cried wolf.

The path to the junkyard had the weakest of glows as the solar lights' power waned. The gate through the fence proved a dark spot that had my hand trembling as I reached to enter the combination to open it. I'd opted for keyless entry so that I wouldn't be that stupid chick in the slasher flicks, who got killed because she dropped the key and couldn't find it in the dark.

The door rattled a bit as I went through, bringing a wince. Had anyone heard? Would anyone take notice? When the wind whistled through the junkyard, metal had a tendency to creak. My entry might not sound out of place.

Tiptoeing in work boots proved difficult. It involved lifting my feet high enough where they wouldn't scuff but also setting them down gently so as not to thud. There were no lights in this area. Not yet. I'd ordered a solar-pow-ered string, but it hadn't arrived yet. One-day delivery, my ass.

I aimed for the office, only to halt as the phone in my pocket vibrated.

Keeping the taser rod in one hand, I pulled out my phone to see that I'd received a new alert. *Motion detected.* The camera that'd spotted it being the one by the garage.

I headed over, moving more quickly with a target. I hesitated just outside the garage-side door, noticing that it wasn't latched all the way. With the roll-down door closed, I had no idea what awaited as the lack of window meant no peeking inside.

My grip on the taser rod grew slippery with sweat. Better not be a hot flash. I kept my thumb on the trigger button for the electricity. Press, swing, and zap! Easy-peasy.

Tell that to the lump in my throat. I took a breath, then another, reminding myself that this was my place. Whoever lurked inside had no business being here.

Only as I kicked open the door did it occur to me that I should have dialed 9-1-1 first. Then, backup would be on its way, at least.

Instead, having already committed to confrontation, I stood framed in the opening, rod pointed outward, facing off against darkness as I yelled, "Don't move, dirtbag!"

Not my best expletive. It didn't receive a reply.

I held my breath as I listened, trying to *see* with my ears. Pure silence met me.

My hand fumbled for the switch I knew to be to my left. As my fingers brushed the plastic-plated edge of it, something brushed past me, cold and startling enough that my hand spasmed as my arm dropped to my side. The rod hit my leg, and the next thing I knew, I lay on the floor, jiggling like a fried egg.

CHAPTER 12

IN GOOD NEWS, I DIDN'T PISS MYSELF. IN OTHER good news, whoever scared the fuck out of me didn't come back to hurt me while I lay stunned on the floor.

World's biggest idiot. I couldn't believe I'd tased myself. At least, there didn't seem to be any long-lasting damage. Eventually, when my muscles decided to belong to me again, I rose to my feet, groaning as I shook out my limbs. Everything appeared to be working okay. Although, I wondered if I'd end up with a white Frankenstein streak in my hair. It happened all the time in the movies.

This time, when my fingers brushed the switch, the light came on, showing my work-shop just as I'd left it, albeit with the bike's frame cleaner than I remembered. Could have sworn I still had lots of degreasing to do—so not important right now.

The strap for the taser pulled on my wrist, and I twisted my lips at the sight of it. So much for protecting myself. I tugged it off and lay it on my workbench. Only to grab it again a second later. Whoever had slammed into me might still be outside. The lights in the garage would render me sightless until my eyes adjusted to the darkness, giving the intruder an advantage if they'd stuck around.

Was it one of the tweakers from last week?

And how had they gotten into the garage without busting the lock? As I neared the door, I eyed the deadbolt. I'd locked it before leaving earlier. I didn't recall seeing any damage when at the door. No one but I knew the combination or had the spare key. Had I failed to latch it properly?

I clutched the pepper spray in my hand as the rod once again dangled from my wrist. The moment I swung open the door, I sprayed wildly and covered my face with the crook of my arm in case of blowback.

When I didn't hear screaming, I peeked and

then blinked. For one, no intruder lurked out-side. And, secondly, dawn crested.

Given the sun rose just before six, almost three hours had passed since I'd left the house to check on things. A long time. I must have passed out completely and not just been dazed from the taser.

Damn.

Pity I didn't feel more rested. Exhausted, I eyed my gates and thought...fuck it. My dog was very happy that I chose to spend the entire morning and the afternoon in bed.

I'd completely detached from the world when my doorbell rang. I ignored it. I was in no shape to answer. I wore the T-shirt and track pants I'd slept in. My hair hadn't been brushed. I'd eaten Cheetos for a late lunch and had the orange fingers to prove it.

All to say, I'd forgotten that the detective was coming over.

Knock. Knock. "Allie?"

I heard his voice and froze. How could I have forgotten?

Blame the tasering. I rushed to the door and apologized as I turned the thumb bolt. "Sorry. Worked late. Why don't you make yourself comfortable while I shower?"

"Actually, I'm here to ask you a few questions."

"Wait, questions about what?" I paused, rather than letting him in.

"Can you open the door? I'd rather discuss this face-to-face."

What if I didn't? I glanced at my outfit. Cringed at my orange fingertips. Love me. Love me when I dressed like I couldn't afford to replace the T-shirt with its tomato sauce stain and the trackpants with the hole in the knee.

I flung open the door in all my crusty beauty.

The grim expression that met me indicated that Brayden had returned to being a detective. "May I come in?"

"Depends. You here to arrest me for something?"

"Don't be ridiculous. You're not a danger to anybody."

I didn't know if I should be pleased or insulted. "Why do you seem so frazzled?"

"Because someone was murdered last night. Someone on the force."

"Oh, shit, that sucks." Trite words because I

didn't actually know what to say. "Were you close?"

"No. It's important because of how they were killed."

A chill filled me, even as I knew what he'd say.

"Someone used a triple claw to rip out their throats."

"Sounds like you have a copycat."

A hopeful reply dashed as he said, "Forensics has already matched it to the weapon used in the original murders. It seems Mahoney might be back."

CHAPTER 13

"MAHONEY, BACK IN TOWN? THAT HARDLY SEEMS likely. He's been gone more than ten years. Why come back now?" I threw the detective's words back at him.

"I don't know," he muttered. "It makes no sense."

For some reason, I thought of my dream. "Could he have returned because of his sister?"

A sharp gaze turned on me. "What sister?"

Oh, shit. How much should I admit? He'd laugh at me for sure if I mentioned my dreams. "I thought I read he had a sister. Special needs. Lived in a home in Ottawa? Part of the reason he lived in the area." I gave him what I knew without indicating where I'd gotten the info.

This was where I'd be told in no uncertain terms that Mahoney didn't have—

"I wasn't aware he had a sibling. Or that he'd care if he did. But it's possible, given his mother remarried when he was still fairly young." Brayden rubbed his chin. A man more into solving the mystery than me. Kind of miffing.

"Now that you've got a lead, why don't you go follow it?" The suggestion emerged on a sour note.

He glanced at me and then finally saw me, offering a rueful grin. "Sorry. I got thrown for a loop when I realized the murderer used the same weapon. It didn't help that I immediately thought of you."

"Me?" Not exactly the kind of thing a woman wanted to hear after a man saw a dead body.

Apparently, my expression alerted him to the fact that he might have said the wrong thing.

Brayden struck, quick as a viper, and grabbed my hands. "I don't want anything to happen to you, Allie. You're special, and it would kill me to see you hurt."

"Uh, thanks?" I honestly didn't have a clue
what to think of his statement. Sexy or creepy?
After all, we'd only just barely met.

"I'm coming on too strong, aren't I?"

"It's okay." Not really. I tugged my hands
free of Mr. Touchy Feely. Yes, I might have
climbed him like a tree before, but today, I
wasn't feeling it. Blame my rough night.

"Can you also forgive me for forgetting to
bring food?" he sheepishly apologized.

"Don't feel bad. I forgot about dinner en-
tirely." The brutal truth. Blame my don't-give-a
-fuck forties. I'd come into mine later than
most. Now, I made up for lost time by being
brutally honest. I no longer wanted to waste
time playing word games.

He didn't take offense. "Understandable.
Given the trauma you endured, I can totally
get how it slipped your mind."

Now I felt like an asshole. "Don't apologize.
I'm being bitchy because I'm tired. I didn't
sleep well."

"Nightmares?" he asked, his expression
pinched with concern.

Given I had no intention of explaining how
I'd gone to check out an intruder on my own

and then accidentally zapped myself, I shrugged and said, "Yup. I might need to look into something to help me sleep."

"I can recommend a good CBD oil blend."

I blinked at the incongruity of a detective offering to tell me about some good weed. I'd still not quite adjusted my mind to the fact that Canada had legalized marijuana. "I think I'll stick to warm milk and honey for now."

The corner of his mouth lifted. "If you change your mind, let me know. I keep some in my nightstand for the rough nights."

The admission cocked my head in query. "What makes you sleepless?"

"Everything. The world is a crime-riddled place, and it's hard not to feel as if I'm not making a dent." He'd moved away from me, and his shoulders slumped.

It felt remarkably raw for him to admit this. "I think you are doing your damnedest to make a difference."

He snorted. "I haven't even found the guys who attacked you."

"But you're trying. And I appreciate it." I flirted with him in all my slobbish glory.

Rather than eye my grungy ensemble, he

stared at my lips. "I really shouldn't. I'm in the middle of an active investigation."

"We don't need long," I teased before nipping his chin.

His arms came around me. "I'll seem like a huge jerk when I have to leave right after."

"Would you feel better if I kicked you out?"

That quirked his lips. "No."

I kissed him and felt the struggle in his frame. I sighed and stepped away. "Fine. Go. But keep in mind that I'm going to start getting a complex if this keeps happening."

"Maybe I should—?" He might have stayed if his phone hadn't buzzed. He muttered a string of expletives that spanned both the English and French languages. *Way to be bilingual.* He offered me a brief, hard kiss before leaving with a promise. "Tomorrow. I don't know what time. But tomorrow for sure."

He left, and I touched my lips. The tingle in them pleased me. The arousal also left me restless. I leashed the cowardly Blade to walk over to my shop despite it being after dark. My big scaredy pup might not defend, but he'd try to escape something fierce if he sensed anything. I had him tethered around my waist and double-fisted my pepper spray.

I encountered nothing on my way to the garage, where I spent the evening and a bit of the night cleaning parts. I didn't even realize I'd closed my eyes until I woke in a hospital.

CHAPTER 14

"WHAT THE FUCK?" I SHOVED MY WAY TO A sitting position, noticing the IV in my arm but no bandages this time. Yay? Seemed premature to celebrate the lack of physical wounds. I shouldn't be here.

Before I could start slamming the button to call the nurse, the door to my room opened, and Brayden peeked in. "You're awake. Finally. I was getting worried."

That made two of us. I'd hate to make waking up in the hospital my thing.

"What happened? What am I doing here?"

"You had an accident."

"What?" I squeaked. "What broke?" Must have been some hefty drugs to hide where I'd been hurt. I slapped my body as he entered the room and eased the door shut.

"Nothing broken. Gas leak. You're lucky I found you when I did. Exposed for a little longer, and we wouldn't be talking."

I paused my frantic slapping of my body to blink at him. "Wait, I passed out due to gas?" Hopefully, not the kind that came out of my butt because I'd die of embarrassment. "Is this Blade's fault?" He did have smelly farts.

Brayden didn't smile at my lame attempt at humor. "Faulty propane valve on your space heater, according to the fire department. I took the liberty of having someone fix it for you."

"Thanks. Wow." Suddenly dizzy, I pressed the control to raise the bed enough that I could lay against my pillow, which barely merited the name. Flat pancake covered in fabric. Useless thing. I wanted my pillow.

"Hey, you okay? Should I call the nurse?"

Oops. My lower lip jutted, and he noticed enough that he wanted to take care of me in the worst way possible. A nurse would poke me and ask me questions. Fuck that. I wanted answers. "How long was I out?"

His shoulders lifted and dropped. "Not

sure. I didn't find you until the morning when I stopped by with coffee and a donut."

"How did you get in?" I hadn't unlocked the main gate.

"Side entrance. When I noticed your junk-yard shut tight, I tried the house. Got worried when you didn't answer, especially since your car was in the driveway and I saw your curtain twitching."

"That would be my dog." Which would be odd because I could have sworn I'd taken the dog with me.

"I know that now, but at the time, I assumed something more nefarious and kicked in the door. Before you freak out, I already had someone fix that, too. When I didn't find you inside, I went looking for you—with the help of your pooch."

"A good thing. Although, I am surprised my dog helped. Usually, he hides at the sight of strangers." Only one thing niggled. Again, I could have sworn I'd brought him with me to the garage. Hard to tell for sure with my mind kind of fuzzy, though.

"Your pooch was worried. We both were."

I rubbed at my face, trying to scrub away

the lingering grogginess. "When can I get out of here?"

"Probably not until tomorrow. They'll want to ensure you've recovered before releasing you."

"But Blade—"

"Is fine," he interrupted. "Once the paramedics grabbed you, I called a guy I know to fix the doorframe that I busted. While he repaired that, I packed you a change of clothes and your purse for when you got discharged." He waved a hand at a chair with the aforementioned pile. "I also fed your dog and took him for a walk. Or, you could say he took me. I got dragged into the run-off ditch not once but three times, for no reason."

"He's a bit skittish."

"A bit?" He arched an incredulous brow. "Your dog practically leapt into my arms when a bird swooped. Thought I'd have to carry him back to your house at one point when something rustled in the bushes."

I smothered a giggle to reply. "The world can be scary."

His snort and head shake said otherwise. "I've never met a dog afraid of his own shadow."

This time, I couldn't hide my grin. "Admit it. He's kind of cute."

"Just a little." Brayden's lips quirked. "But a cat is better."

My turn to make a disparaging noise. "No way."

"Yes, way. Maybe I'll have to prove it to you by finding a kitten who doesn't terrify your dog."

"We both know my dog will be terrified even if you find a baby kitty smaller than he shits." Eloquent I was not; and yet he smiled.

"I guess we'll find out."

I liked his use of *we*. "Thanks for taking time out of your day to visit me. I know you're busy."

"If I'd been less busy, you wouldn't have been in your workshop the night your equipment turned faulty."

Someone was pretty sure of himself. "Are you implying I'd have let you stay the night? Sounds kind of risky. How do I know you don't snore?" I teased.

"I do, but planned to leave you too tired to notice."

His sharp riposte had me laughing and

then groaning as I grabbed my head. "Oh, that hurts."

Instant apology creased his expression. "Sorry. I should let you rest."

He moved off the edge of my bed, and I grabbed at him. "Please, don't. I'd like it if you stayed." Being with him helped me ignore the fact that I'd landed back in a hospital. At least, this time, it was an accident.

"I'm supposed to be going over case files," he started, only to halt. Then he said, "Give me ten minutes. I'll be right back."

He left too quickly for me to ask anything. A part of me honestly didn't expect him to return, especially as the ten minutes on the clock hanging on the wall ticked close to fifteen. They'd placed me in a room by myself, which made me wonder at my luck. I had no insurance, which meant I could probably expect a hefty bill. Free Canadian healthcare didn't come with luxuries like privacy in the hospital. Cable television, a room to myself, and other things meant to make a person more comfortable all had a price.

At seventeen minutes, Brayden reappeared, holding quite the armful. He had a portfolio shoved under an arm, a tray of drinks, a bag that emitted a delightful aroma, and a stuffed gray cat.

My mouth rounded in surprise as he shoved it at me. "Here's a kitty to get you used to the idea."

It was stupid and corny, and I loved it. I tucked the cat close as he then showed me the contents of the paper bag.

"If the nurse asks, lie and say I didn't share," he whispered, glancing at the closed door.

Biting deep into a burger, I could only grunt in agreement. Hungrier than expected, I stuffed my face with the burger and fries, which I swore tasted like Heaven. Or maybe it was the company that made it all better.

As I inhaled my food, Brayden regaled me with more tales of his epic walk with Blade, which turned out to be a lot of pulling, yanking, and dragging—of the human.

I started laughing until I gasped for air. "Stop," I pleaded.

He did, but only to wait until I finished eating before waxing eloquently about the size of my dog's shit. "It was literally larger than a cat. Which, speaking of, you know we can get a litter box that cleans the waste for you each time it goes. All you gotta do is take out the bag each week."

"But will a cat smother and lick me until I beg for mercy?"

"It might sit on your face to suffocate you while you sleep," he offered.

Which led to more giggling as I sipped on the iced tea he'd brought. Good choice. Not too sweet, cold and refreshing, with ice chunks I could crunch.

After he'd cleared the meal, I caught sight of the last thing he'd brought.

"What's that?" I asked, pointing to the leather portmanteau, the brown exterior battered and scored.

"Case files. Remember how I said I was supposed to be looking them over?" He eyed me. "Congrats, I'm deputizing you as my aid."

"Won't you get in trouble for showing me police files?"

"Not if I claim I required your services as an outside consultant."

"You can do that?"

"As long as I don't submit a bill, they won't bother asking questions."

"What's the case you're working on?" I

couldn't help but ask, intrigued as he pulled out folders thick with paper.

"You are looking at the police reports for the Triclaw Murders that happened over a decade ago. Given the recent seeming appearance of one, I want to go over the old case files and compare them against each other."

I perked right up. "Because you think Mahoney is back."

"I don't want to jump to conclusions without evidence."

"I understand, but you surely have some idea. What do you think?"

"That someone is killing people, and we need to find them." The correct thing for a cop to say.

"Where do we start?" I rubbed my hands.

He hesitated. "Are you sure? The pics and descriptions can be gruesome. Maybe this wasn't a good idea."

"Is that supposed to deter me? I watch crime shows all the time. I blame my youthful love of Scooby-Doo and the gang."

His lips quirked. "I doubt we're looking for a ghost, in this case."

Funny thing was, Scooby and the gang only

rarely found a supernatural reason by the end of each episode. A person usually ended up being the one perpetuating the evil.

Despite a scolding from my nurse, Brayden and I spent the next few hours poring over case files. He'd not exaggerated when he'd called it grim reading.

The victims all those years ago had all died similarly, meaning a triple blade slicing them open. For some, the bleed-out happened quickly as the slash went across the throat and the severed jugular pumped the body dry. Others got it in the gut, the evisceration spilling their intestines, a deadly wound that took longer to kill, meaning they suffered before they died.

The one thing they all had in common?

"The killer only ever went after really shitty people," I observed after the first four files showed the victims with lengthy arrest records.

"Even shitty people deserve justice. It's not up to a vigilante to be judge and executioner. And not all the victims were criminals. Two people don't fit the profile." He handed me two files. One for a college girl working at a

EVE LANGLAIS

bar on the weekends, and the other for a young
man—a paramedic who'd stopped on his way
home to help someone overdosing and had
paid with his life.

They did seem oddly out of place.

"What about the newest one?" I'd not yet
looked at the file.

"You have to promise not to say a word
about what you see," he cautioned.

"Swear." I crossed my heart, and he handed
over the file.

Flipping it open, my brows rose. "The most
recent victim really was a cop."

"Not just any cop, but someone who
worked on the Mahoney case way back when."

"Could be a coincidence. Or—" As all the
crime shows I'd ever watched suddenly turned
on my super suspicious brain, I blurted, "The
killer is back, and he's out to get those who
tried to capture him. Which would implicate
Mahoney. But what if the killer isn't Mahoney,
and they're pissed that you got it wrong all
those years ago?"

"That's a lot of conjecture."

"So, what's your theory?" I sassed. At least,
I'd come up with some ideas.

"The one thing you didn't mention. That

the Trikillz gang has resurrected in Ottawa. Borenson, the guy we found dead, was also part of the drug squad for a while. He might have been the first to spot their return, and they tried to silence him."

My nose wrinkled. "How does that make more sense? By silencing him with the three slashes, they announced their presence."

"Or did someone want to pin it on them to divert attention? Once we figure out the motive, we'll have a direction for a suspect."

"Where should we start checking first?"

"Me, not we. I am going to leave you now to get some sleep and check in on your dog. He's due for a walk. I'm hoping not to get dragged into a cornfield and left for dead."

"Blade is scared of cornfields, but not thickets. Wear long sleeves." At his expression, I chuckled and explained that no walk was necessary given the dog run in my back yard.

"What if I want to walk him?" was his riposte.

To which, I laughed and said, "You like him. Maybe there's hope for you yet."

"Maybe." He dropped a kiss on my lips. "I'll see you tomorrow. Get a good night's sleep."

I'd sleep better in my bed. And why shouldn't I? I felt fine. I couldn't believe the nurse didn't believe me and insisted that I take a nap. What I wanted was more food. It took some cajoling to get the nurse to agree.

By the time it arrived, I'd fallen asleep.

CHAPTER 15

I SLEPT THE WHOLE NIGHT THROUGH, NOT EVEN A single dream. I woke hungry. Then disappointed. Breakfast sucked. The shower the nurse arranged did much for my morale, though. Around lunchtime, the hospital agreed to release me. To my surprise and delight, Brayden brought me home from the hospital, having illegally parked in front of the main doors. Being OPP had its uses.

He drove and told me how he'd become pals with Blade, who avoided ditches on their latest walk, but did ensure that he stepped in fresh shit.

"My shoe is ruined. Which sucks. I suffered a blister getting those heels broken in."

I understood his pain. "He's an asshole. Good thing he's cute."

"Good thing." Brayden snorted.

He left me tucked on the couch, literally. He grabbed a blanket from the closet and wrapped it around me, leaving with a promise to return for dinner.

I napped the moment he left. When I woke, I ate and then slept again with my dog—best day ever for him. I awoke again later feeling refreshed, especially after my shower, where I spent time updating my shaved bits.

My legs and pits had reached the bristly point. My pubes, however, were short enough that I wasn't risking a rash.

Brayden arrived before six, bearing two souvlaki platters consisting of seasoned meat on a stick, salad, and rice. Delicious. He also tossed in a movie, some alien cop drama that tried to be funny but failed. And the only reason I could state the horrid execution with certainty? I watched it rather than having the sex I wanted.

Important to note that it wasn't because of a lack of desire on either of our parts. The chemistry between us was off the charts. Last time, his phone had cock-blocked him. Whereas, this time, my cunt—and I meant that in the most derogatory way—ensured I wasn't getting any.

Forget menopause. Apparently, my periods weren't done with me yet. Six months of dryness and it chose to hit me now, the horrifying and very red Crotch Falls. Within minutes of our kissing, the cramps hit, and I had to excuse myself.

In the bathroom, I dropped my track pants —my cleanest, nicest pair that had plenty of room for him to shove his hand in. Quick to remove, as well. They hit the floor, and so did the underwear that appeared as if Dexter used it as a drop cloth. A good thing I kept clean pairs in the bathroom. I'd had too many episodes of night sweats to *not* keep extra clothes in here.

I had to dig in the cupboard for a tampon. Six months of liberty ruined! I should have been done with it. Given the roiling of my lower belly, I added a pad. Layered up, I grimaced. So much for making out and a movie.

Once I emerged, I hit the kitchen to serve up some popcorn. The bowl set between us gave me space. I expected him to ask me what was wrong. To try and kiss me.

The fucker didn't push at all.

So, I mauled him, tasting the butter on his lips as his hands settled on my hips.

Mmm. My pussy flexed. The wetness I felt didn't come from desire.

"I'll be right back." I vacillated between frustration and annoyance. I was probably being paranoid. No way I'd gone through a tampon already. It had been like half an hour, maybe forty-five minutes.

Despite my precautions, my underpants got murdered again. The pad fought valiantly to contain the flow and failed—bloody literal hell.

It took me a few minutes to clean up, put in the dusty menstrual cup—relax, I rinsed it first —then yank on new clean undies layered with a thick pad. Then, over that, a less reputable pair of dark track pants. When I emerged, I reminded myself there was nothing wrong with my body. Menses was a natural part of life.

My date waited on the couch, one arm over the back, his expression smoldering as he watched my return.

So unfair. I wanted nothing more than to jump his bones. Alas, I bluntly put an end to it. "So…bad news. Aunt Flo is visiting."

You have company? Since when?" He appeared genuinely puzzled.

How could a guy exist who didn't know what that meant? "Aunt Flo is code speak for my period. As in my time of the month. When the cavern of sensual delights bleeds for several days. Understand? Or do we need to go into the whole narrative about how a uterus works?" My embarrassment in having to explain it all made me harsher than intended.

Poor guy blushed. "I understand."

Adorable, but I forged on, lest he not think me so cute if he caught a horrifying glimpse of what was coming out of me.

"While Flo is visiting, there will be no touching below my waist, and before you say you're okay with a little bit of blood, I'm not. It's gross."

The ruddiness in his cheeks deepened. "I would never dream of asking."

"Why not? Don't you like me?" I was suddenly PMS-ing hard and needed to know.

His lips twitched. "I like you very much. Enough to know when the time is right, it will happen."

Would it? Because I swear, it was as if fate conspired against us. Would we ever have sex? I hoped so because if the foreplay kept up, a slight breeze might just make me come.

I needed distraction, and the shitty movie didn't offer it. The terrible dialogue couldn't hold a candle to the hot dude sitting beside me. The feel of his leg under my hand—because look at that, after all my fine words, I groped *him*. The problem being, while I could totally jerk him to climax, it would lead to frustration for me.

I snatched back my hand and glanced away in time to see an alien on screen swallowing someone whole. "How's the case going? Any more dead bodies?"

"No." *Buzz.* His phone went off, and I swore I must have had a premonition because I knew what he'd say next.

"Fuck me. They think they found another one. I have to go."

Another? "Of course, you do. You need to get there while the crime scene is still fresh for clues." Clues he'd hopefully share with me.

"Are you sure? Will you be okay?" His concern warmed me.

"Yes, I'll be fine. Go," I shooed him. "If you're not here, then I can stop wearing pants and stuff my face with salty chips."

"You could have taken your pants off anytime," he said with a wink. "And I like chips."

"I don't share when I PMS." Get between me and the salt, and you'd get stabbed with whatever I had handy.

The Jerk had gotten tined by a fork a week after he'd asked me for a divorce and thought he could touch my chips. Mocking him soundly for whining meant he didn't call the cops. To this day, I still didn't feel bad.

I'd been more careful to control myself after that. My unrequited rage issues needed a tight leash.

Brayden leaned in for a kiss. "If you're sure."

"I'm sure," I murmured against his mouth.

He gave me a squeeze and then stepped away, saying, "I'll be by tomorrow if I can."

"Bring donuts if it's before dinner. At least a half-dozen."

"As my lady commands." He chuckled as he left.

What an adorable man. I hated my plumbing for ruining what should have been an orgasmic date.

It still being early, I tried watching television. Nothing held my interest. I tackled Blade and took care of his burrs, which led to him sighing.

"Next time, don't run through the prickly shit," I chided as I pulled out the fourth one.

I thought about going to bed. That would never work with the amount of nervous energy filling my limbs. Too much napping today, and it had begun to filter through that I'd almost died.

Propane gas leak. How had I not noticed? Propane had an additive that gave it a putrid smell, a warning for people to avoid poisoning. I should have noticed unless I'd been sleeping so soundly that it'd never registered.

Since when did I fall asleep in the garage, though? I'd always made it back to bed before. The last thing I recalled was working on the bike while my dog slept in the chair. Yet the detective had claimed that Blade was in the house.

Had my dog left the garage? How, with the door closed? And his doggy one at the house had been left sealed, as well. It made no sense unless I hadn't brought Blade. Maybe I'd just *thought* I had. The same way I kept thinking that I was talking to Mahoney.

As if thinking of him conjured his voice, I heard him say: *That leak wasn't an accident.*

What?

I whirled and blinked. I was alone but for my dog. He stretched on the couch and let one rip. Having been through the gagging before, I immediately lifted the collar of my shirt over my mouth and headed for the front door.

I didn't even know I planned to leave until the shoes were on my feet. Apparently, I was going out. I wanted to see the garage and the leaky valve. Reassure myself. An accident made sense. Murder didn't. Who would want to kill me?

Given the hour, I grabbed my red sweater before clucking my tongue. "Coming?" I asked my dog as I stood at the front door, eyeballing the cans of pepper spray. I ended up grabbing one for each hand.

Blade stood at the far end of the living room and whined.

"I know it's dark. You don't have to come. I just want a quick peek."

The mournful noise almost changed my mind.

"Get the bed warm for me, baby. I'll be right back."

Closing and locking the front door, I moved quickly from my property to the fence, then the garage, setting off two cameras on my path.

Only as I punched in my code did I pause to wonder how Brayden had gotten inside to save me. He'd told me about fixing the door to my house, which he'd admitted to kicking in. But what of this one? It didn't appear busted.

Could it be that, feeling the poison, I'd tried to escape and opened the door, only to collapse? It would explain how my dog had gotten out, and Brayden had gotten in.

The side door to the garage opened easily, and I entered but hesitated before flipping on the switch. Gas and electricity didn't mix. I took a big sniff and detected nothing. The rotten-egg smell of propane and natural gas was distinctive. Still, just in case, I headed for the roll-up door and heaved it high. It exposed me, but at least I could be assured of breathing fresh air. Only then did I finally turn on the lights.

Blinded by the sudden brightness, I blinked before I could glance around for the supposed leaky valve. Few things used propane in this space. I kept a few hand torches but those didn't have enough in a canister to hurt. The only other thing that used gas was the heating unit for the garage, mounted into the wall for easy venting. I moved my fingers over the compact furnace with the ductwork sprawling out from it in a metal trifecta of conduits.

Someone had capped off the unit's gas connection, and the red tag read today's date with a brief description of the problem. *Faulty hose.* Didn't sound like attempted murder to me. More like simple maintenance. Never mind the fact that I'd had the fucking thing serviced when I bought the place. Could be rodents had gotten to the gas line, or maybe I'd gotten a faulty hose. It happened.

Turning from the furnace, my gaze fell on the bike, looking even further along than I recalled. It truly went together like a dream. I barely remembered rebuilding the motor.

Once my eyes hit the bike, I had to approach, admiring the metallic sheen that had emerged from the filth. Not the silvery gray as expected. Even cleaned, the composition remained dark. A neat trick that seemed to preclude a need for paint.

I ran my fingers over the slick lines of it, impressed. In no time at all, I'd be ready to fire up the engine. I only waited on a few parts, the seat being the most important because I'd not found any damage other than a need for a good cleaning and oiling.

EVE LANGLAIS

The wolf head hood at the front of the bike offered a menacing countenance that, like the body, didn't appear to require paint. The dark metallic sheen was already glossy. Its lines sleek.

Riding it would be a rush. I couldn't wait.

The bike remained firmly clamped, so I had no qualms about straddling it. The lack of a cushioned seat meant the bracket pushed against my crotch as I gingerly crouched and gripped the bars. At the contact, there was an instant tingle. I tilted my head back and relaxed. Tried to imagine the motor purring and the wind on my visor—not my face because the law said I had to wear a bobblehead helmet. Once I bought one. I'd hated all the styles I'd seen thus far.

The gruff yet familiar voice jolted. "Get off the bike. Can't you see I'm working on it?"

144

CHAPTER 16

HOW COULD I BE DREAMING? I'D JUST CLOSED MY eyes. No way had I fallen asleep sitting on the bare frame of the bike.

A glance showed me still sitting on the bracket and Mahoney scowling at me, part of the bike in his hands. The next piece to go on, as a matter of fact.

"Why won't you go away?" I complained.

"I could say the same." He crouched and ignored me to reattach the clamp that I'd pulled off days before.

"What are you doing?" I asked as he went back for another piece.

"Putting my bike together."

"That's my project." A petulant reply.

"Wrong, lady. This's my ride."

"You abandoned your ride in the scrapyard. It became mine when I bought it."

"Still persisting in that story?"

"Yes, because it's true. You're just a psychic ghost haunting my dreams because you have an interesting and tragic backstory."

His brows arched almost comically high. "Me, the ghost? You're the one who isn't real."

I sighed. "You can be as convincing as you like. I'm not stupid. You're part of my subconscious and its anxiety at the fact that someone's decided to murder people the same way you once did."

"Is that a fact?"

"Even if you didn't, doesn't matter. It's happening again. And if it's not you, then maybe Brayden is right, and it's the work of your old gang."

"Impossible."

"How would you know?"

"Because every member of Trikillz is dead. I am the last one."

"Are you? How do you know they're all gone?"

"I just do."

"Well, maybe you're wrong. After all, people around here thought you'd croaked, too." Knowing I dreamed and technically argued with myself didn't stop me from stating it.

"I think I'd know if I died," he opined.

"If you say so. What about your gang? How did they bite the big one? I thought some of them were in prison."

"They were taken out behind bars. "

"How? Rival gang retaliation?"

He snorted. "No one would dare."

"Don't be so sure. From what I heard, your gang was pretty hardcore. You must have had many enemies."

"Perhaps." He shrugged. "I wouldn't know, since I got out."

"Did you? Maybe they didn't want to let you go so you killed them."

He arched a brow. "Why would I do that? I quit the gang. That didn't stop them from being my friends."

"I find that hard to believe."

"Listen, lady, don't you think if I was a killer, I would have ended your annoying questions a while ago?"

"*I'm* annoying?" I almost shrieked. "You're the guy who keeps showing up inside my head, bossing me around."

"Oh, no, you don't. You are not flipping this around." He jabbed a finger in my direction. "You are the one who keeps invading my spaces. Go away. Play your seductive games with someone else."

I had to admire how my dream version of Mahoney had such autonomy. Felt so real. Until he claimed seduction. Ha. He wasn't anything close to my type with his square, rugged looks and abrasive manner. The kind of guy who liked it rough.

Mmm...

A cramp hit me, and I glared at my stomach. Couldn't I escape the period from Hell even in sleep? Another spasm hit me, along with a gush of wet heat between my legs.

"You've got to be fucking kidding me." It was like being fifteen again, wearing white jeans to school, and my period deciding to come five days early.

Then, as now, it went through fabric and stained. In this case, the bike bracket. Back then? My seat in class. Everybody saw it. I became Bloody Allie, and people said my name seven times while slamming locker doors when I went by. I wore that name for two years until Patricia, a grade under me, had it happen on a recreational class trip to the pool. The pink water had the boys screaming, "shark." And after that, guess what theme song got hummed when Patricia passed by.

When I swung my leg to get off the bike, the metal strut I'd been straddling glistened with my menses as if I wore nothing to halt it. So gross. I made it a few steps to grab a shop towel before the spins hit, and I had to kneel on the floor.

"What's wrong with you?" Mahoney barked and yet crouched beside me, a heavy hand on my shoulder to steady me.

"I think I might have overdone it." My release from the hospital didn't mean I'd completely recovered.

"You need to lie down. Where do you live?" Was that actual concern from my Neanderthal biker?

"Ha, ha. Funny. You know where I live. And before you say that bed in the house next door is yours, my pink and purple comforter begs to disagree."

He opened and shut his mouth before shaking his head. "I give up. You're crazy.

"And tired." I yawned. "I don't suppose you could carry me?" After all, my dream version of Mahoney had him even bulkier than Brayden. What would the detective think if he knew I kept dreaming of his nemesis?

What would he do if he found out I'd fallen asleep in the garage again? Waking up would have sucked if I'd face-planted from the bike.

Mahoney swung me into his arms.

"What are you doing?" I squeaked, grabbing at his shoulders.

"Carrying you, as bitched."

"Not bitched. I asked. If you don't want to, put me down," I complained out of a sense of obligation. Fuck the feminist movement right this second. I wanted to be carried for once in my fucking life, even if it was only in a dream.

"Put you down so you can faint and hit your head? I'm sure you'd blame me for that somehow. Or, with my luck, you'd wind up crazier."

"There is nothing wrong with my mind," I grumbled. Other than a hitherto unknown fetish for being carried by borderline barbarian types.

Mahoney strode the path between the junk piles without qualm to the door in the fence. Took me right up to the house, although he did pause to grimace. "Where did those flowers come from?"

"Canadian Tire." I'd bought the hanging arrangement to give my porch some color.

He frowned but didn't reply as he stepped into the house. He kicked the door shut, and while he faltered walking through the living room, took me straight to the bedroom with its promised frilly comforter.

He dumped me on the bed and glanced around. "This isn't my room."

"Not anymore. I repainted." The house I'd bought had been in surprisingly good condition considering how long it had lain vacant. I'd expected to find mold and peeling plaster when I first walked into the place; however, it had been sealed against outside intrusions, and the insulation protected it from most decay.

Or so science would claim. I'd heard someone in the post office mutter that the ghost was what kept the place from falling down.

A ghost named Killian Mahoney, who wandered around the room touching things. My things. Except for the dresser, which he whirled from, stating, "This is mine."

"If you say so." It came with the house.

"I know so." He yanked open the drawers to find my things. "Where's my shit?"

"Your stuff is gone. Long gone, I'd say. By the time I took over the property, there wasn't anything of yours left. No clothes. No pictures. Nothing but a few pieces of furniture and some moldy papers."

"This can't be right." His lips flattened as he exited my bedroom, and I heard startled yelping. Rushing out, I prepared to save my poor puppy, only to halt as the crying abruptly ceased.

"You'd better not have hurt Blade," I exclaimed, popping into the living room to see my dog cautiously approaching Mahoney.

"That's a good boy." He reached out his hand and scratched Blade behind the ears. Must have been a good rub because that back leg started thumping, and the traitor gazed at him with loving eyes.

"What did you do to my dog?" Because Blade never took to people that easily.

"He's a fine beast."

My dog sat straight at the praise.

I threw him under the bus. "When he's not hiding from things that scare him."

"Sometimes, it's smart to hide, so long as

you act when the time comes to do the right thing."

I snorted. "As if an ex-gangbanger would know the right thing."

"The right thing isn't about laws but morals. Things you can live with that let you sleep at night versus things that don't."

"Are there many things that keep you awake?"

"Not anymore. I sleep more than I'd like," he admitted, looking momentarily confused.

"And, apparently, I was more tired than I realized. God, I hope I don't wake up on the shop floor. If Brayden finds me there again..."

"Brayden being the man you haven't had sex with."

"Only because of circumstance. It's going to happen. It's just a matter of when."

"A real lover wouldn't make you wait." He stepped closer, and I had to angle my head to see him.

"He'll wait because he doesn't want his dick to look like something took an ax to it."

Mahoney frowned. "You want to cut off his cock?"

"More like he'll look like it's been murdered if he puts it anywhere near my girl parts. I'm on my period."

"His loss. My gain." He moved in, and I dodged out of reach.

"What part of *I'm on my period* did you not understand?"

Rather than appear repugned, he grinned. "What's a little blood between friends? Nothing a shower can't fix." He put one hand on my lower back, tilting me into him.

I put my hands on his chest and shoved to regain some distance. "Stop acting like you're irresistible."

"Then stop looking at me like you'd enjoy climbing me for a good ride."

"I am not!" I huffed.

"If I put my hand down your pants, wanna bet you'd be wet?"

"Yeah, because I'm fucking bleeding. So, hands off." I moved out of his zone to give myself breathing space. I rubbed my forehead. I really should wake up. Nodding off in the garage couldn't be healthy. What if the lingering gas made me pass out? What if it wasn't safe, and I'd put myself back in danger?

"Let's get you back to bed so I can go." Mahoney tried to steer me in the direction of my bedroom.

"Go where? I thought this was your house?" My sarcastic rejoinder.

"Maybe there is something to what you've told me. At times, it's as if there are things out of reach. Something important I've forgotten..."

"Like why you disappeared?" I prodded as he sat me on the edge of the bed.

"I would have never just left. Not without taking care of Ginny. I have to find her," he muttered before walking through the wall of the house.

Like a fucking ghost.

My stomach cramped, and I glanced down to see the stain on my pants had grown and caught the edge of my sheet. Gross. And I'd been too busy arguing with a dead man to do anything about it.

As I ran water in the bathroom, taking care of the murder scene in my pants, it occurred to me how real this all felt. But it wasn't until I actually woke in my bed the next day, my pants still soaking in the sink, my sheet stripped, and me lying on a towel, that it occurred to me I must have either blanked out coming back from the garage or sleepwalked. Either way, I'd lost time again because no way had Mahoney, ghost or not, carried me.

In other news, according to the internet, yet another body had been found overnight. The third one attributed to the resurrected Triclaw Killer.

I waited all day for Brayden to visit. In the end, I had to settle for the text he sent.

Busy. Miss you. Promise to bring a dozen donuts if I can get free.

Maybe I wouldn't be available. While I understood that his job was important, my petty ass remained less than impressed that work ranked higher than I did.

Then again, not being bothered by the detective left me free time to work on the bike.

Soon, my precious. Soon, we'll be riding.

CHAPTER 17

TWO DAYS PASSED WITH ONLY BRIEF BRAYDEN visits where he arrived bearing donuts—maple cream being his favorite, and mine. The guy also brought me bouquets, not always the store-bought kind. Some were obviously wild and picked from ditches and fields. Each time he popped in, often while I was working, we spent most of it exchanging kisses. My lingering period—whereupon I passed clots that might be cause for concern—made sure we couldn't even indulge in a quickie.

During that time, I worked on the bike, which really needed a name. Even sold some scrap. Why anyone would pay me to take the remains of a minivan, I'd never understand. But it would look good at tax time, proving this was an actual job and not a hobby. Doing something I enjoyed and getting paid for it. It took a midlife upheaval to finally get my ass on the right path.

As much as I enjoyed working on the motorcycle, I never stayed past dark. Not anymore. I'd had enough frights, and I also kept hoping the detective would pop by. He did, but could never stay long. I might have to drop his phone in the toilet one of these days.

Despite my shorter days, each morning when I arrived at the garage, it perturbed me to discover that more of the bike had been put together than I recalled. Meaning, either my memory was faulty, or I'd sleepwalked and repaired it. It would have been plausible if the cameras had noticed me coming and going. Yet every time I checked my surveillance app, it showed no motion detected. Not the human kind, at any rate. Only a single incursion by a fox, which had scared the shit out of me at first. Night-vision shit gave the fox glowing, horror-movie eyes.

Since the idea of losing my marbles bothered me, I ignored it. Mostly because if I went to a doctor and he fixed me, Mahoney would probably stop talking to me. He'd been keeping me company a lot as I worked on the bike. Ghost or imaginary friend, I remained straddling the fence on what to call him. Either way, it wasn't a relationship, no matter how real it felt.

On Thursday, despite being in the home stretch for parts left to install, I actually had to be a junkyard owner. Apparently, word had begun circulating that I dealt in parts, both buying and selling. People called and asked if they could drop off their cars. I took those for free. If they complained and asked for money, I told them they could always drop it off somewhere else, knowing full well that many places charged a disposal fee.

The newer stuff was parked nicely in rows, spaced wide enough apart that people could get inside and strip the interiors if desired. I sold a set of minivan seats, three stereos, and a bumper, all before lunch.

As I munched on some poutine—that I'd paid too much to have delivered—I did the paperwork involved in the morning's sales and acquisitions. I tried to always stay on top because once shit started piling up, it often got too deep too quick, becoming daunting so it only kept getting larger.

The afternoon continued busily, enough that I couldn't repair the compactor, even though the parts had arrived. I really should get it fixed. Once I had it good to go, I could commence cleaning the yard of useless metal and selling bundles of it. Eventually, I hoped to be tower-free, replaced by only neatly lined-up vehicles. It might sound weird, but I also fantasized about finding abandoned wrecks in fields and forests. I'd take them all so someone could experience the thrill of seeing their dream car on my lot and having the satisfaction of bringing it back to its former glory.

Speaking of satisfaction and rebuilding, maybe I should put on my big-girl panties and play with the bike after dinner. At six, I locked the gates and, as I passed the garage, popped my head in to ogle the almost finished beauty. I gaped in surprise at the few remaining pieces left to install. So close to being done. Close enough that I could probably fire up the motor in the next hour.

"I have to eat first." Said aloud as an audible reminder. If I didn't and something went wrong, I knew how I was. I'd be troubleshooting instead of taking care of myself.

Excitement had me jittery. I couldn't shovel

dinner into my mouth fast enough. My dog almost shed a tear in pride at my gluttony, even as he remained the inhaling food champ. I just hoped I didn't hack it up later as he sometimes did...on my bed.

Fucker always puked on fabric. If he started to heave on the tile floor, he'd actually race to the nearest carpet, couch—or his favorite, my bed—to spew.

I felt so special.

Rather than join me, Blade chose to lie on the couch, listening to his favorite movie, the one with the ice princess. I'd learned not to say her name aloud because he lost his mind. Sometimes, he even howled along with the singing.

I threw on my red sweater with its deep hood. A chill in the air spoke of the summer shifting finally into fall, which meant cooler temps at night, and a darkness that fell early.

Hesitating on my threshold, I hugged myself. Did I really want to go out?

As fear filled me, I could have sworn I heard Mahoney whisper, *"Don't be afraid."*

My shoulders straightened. My chin lifted. Since when was I a coward?

I marched to the junkyard and my garage.

Upon entering, I immediately rolled up the main door and then shone a light outside of it. *Ain't no one getting close without me seeing them first.*

The tasing rod hung on a hook, fully charged. A can of pepper spray was within reach of my tools. I had a screwdriver in my back pocket. Although, if given a choice, I'd palm a heavy wrench. Better for bashing heads with.

Only once I'd ensured that my area remained secure did I turn to the motorcycle and the tarp with the few remaining pieces. Less, I could have sworn, than I recalled from before dinner.

I'd already installed the seat I'd ordered and had rapid-shipped. The new wiring for the lights hadn't fixed the jolt I got each time I touched the bike. I'd gotten used to it, though. Enjoyed it, actually. When I got fanciful, I imagined it was the bike talking to me, guiding me, happy that someone lavished it with love.

"Almost there, sweetheart," I murmured to the bike. I got to work, putting in the last of the pieces, then moved on to the adding and checking of fluids. Only two things left before I could take it on a maiden run.

I rolled the tires, already on rims, into position and attached them. Checked over the brakes, hesitating to call it done. Had I missed anything?

"It's ready."

His voice. Yet *my* hands released the pressure to lower the lift. I unstrapped the bike and held it for a moment to admire.

It was a damned fine-looking machine. Without paint, the metal should have been matte and dull, yet it shone. Sleek to the touch. The wolf face was finely wrought. The bulbs for its eyes had been replaced. Given I didn't want to get ticketed, I'd had to stick with regular white and not the red that would have been cooler. Although, the turn signal that flashed crimson from inside its eye socket did somewhat make up for it.

Both the front and rear fenders swooped and ended in three sharp tines. Coincidence or a remnant of Mahoney's Trikillz days?

The handlebars fit into my grip as if sized for me, which made no sense given that Mahoney had me by several inches.

Straddling the seat, I sighed in comfort at the padding I'd chosen for the black leather stitched cushion. My period had slowed down enough that a pad contained it, so hopefully I wouldn't ruin the expensive splurge on my first ride.

Despite the fact that I lacked a helmet, I rolled the bike out of the garage, snaring a pair of safety goggles as I passed. I wouldn't go far, only a little ride to see how it ran. Not the two-lane highway in front of my place, but the side road on the east side. With it being after dark, not many would see me. I'd draw my hood down over my brow to hide my features. A lack of a license plate meant cops couldn't run them to grab a name. I'd be anonymous.

How daring. The thick bike between my legs felt good.

For a second, I could have sworn I heard Mahoney whisper, *"I'd feel better."*

"I prefer my lovers to have an actual body," I muttered as I squeezed the gas and booted the kickstart to get the motorcycle going.

At first, nothing happened. Not even a choke. Then, on the next try, a small rumble. The third kick was the charm. It uttered a vibrating growl. I quickly fed it gas, and the beast roared to life.

Glory, praise be.

Shall we go for a ride?

This time, I swore the voice came from the bike. I didn't care. "Hell, yeah."

The motorcycle leaped forward as if possessed by a wild mind of its own. I clung tightly in surprise, my hands wrapped around the handle grips, my thighs squeezing the seat and frame. The rumble didn't disappoint.

Even at low speed, it didn't take long to reach the front gate where Mahoney stood, the lock in his hand.

"Don't go far," he admonished as he pushed open the barrier.

I blinked at the apparition, and really hoped I wasn't dreaming of this ride, or about to crash into a closed gate.

Taking in a breath, I leaned down, gunned the bike, and off we flew.

CHAPTER 18

THE BIKE HANDLED BETTER THAN I COULD HAVE hoped for. Smooth to shift, easy to ride. Everything about it was perfect. There was only one thing I'd need to fix before my next outing.

My clothes.

My red hoodie couldn't completely cut out the wind and chill. It ripped through the fabric and stiffened my limbs. An easy enough thing to rectify. I'd invest in a proper jacket, maybe even some dedicated boots and chaps if I planned to ride regularly.

Wait, was I keeping the bike?

Why not? It hadn't cost me much in parts and only a bit of my time, plus I really liked it. Although, next time, along with goggles, I should tie back my hair. I tucked it into my hood and then put the goggle strap over it to hold it in place. I really needed better equipment because this was hardly my most attractive look.

As I wheeled around, heading back for the junkyard, the bike chose to misbehave. It didn't spin or stall out. Nope. It decided it wanted to shoot across the road, zip through a shallow ditch, and then fire off towards the woods. We emerged by some train tracks. The bumpy gravel had my teeth chattering as I cursed.

"What the fuck? Why won't you turn?" I couldn't get the bike to obey me at all. Letting go of the gas accomplished nothing. It was as if it drove itself.

Currently, it aimed for a bridge, the overpass allowing the train to flow under while the road for cars and other vehicles crossed above. Against the curved wall of the tunnel a barrel spewed flame.

The bike slowed that I might see a group of people standing over the barrel. They had a similar zombie-like sway to their bodies as they stared as if hypnotized by the flames.

Their gaunt faces looked demonic in the dancing flamelight. Hair mostly greasy, unbrushed, except for the one who'd shaved it to the scalp. Their eyes lacked focus. One still had a rubber band hose wrapped around his biceps, loose but ready to tighten for the needle.

Tweakers. A bunch of them and not something I wanted to deal with. I had no plans to stop until I saw one of my attackers.

Skinny, the one who'd held me down as his friend tried to rape me. The rage hit me suddenly, and I bent low over the bike as I aimed for him. It took all those around the barrel a moment to notice me, their blasting metal tunes drowning out the sound of the engine.

When they finally realized I bore down with singular intent, they scattered with screams. Although, one guy nodded and yelled, "And you shall know they are death by the steel wolf that they ride."

Not the exact quote but I liked it.

Skinny turned out to be a runner. I gladly chased, bumping the bike over the gravel lining the path the rail bisected. When he veered into the woods, I remained close behind, humping over rutted ground, the roots only partially submerged.

Eventually, Skinny flipped around and got caught in the beams of light. He screamed, "Don't hurt me."

Until he asked, I actually didn't know what I would do. Might not have a choice as the bike appeared in charge. It stopped advancing a few feet from Skinny, who backed into a tree.

"Fuck off!" he yelled, crossing his arms over his eyes to block out my headlights.

"The same way you fucked off the night you beat on a woman?" A feminist would be pleased to be treated like a man, but at the same time, what they'd attempted to do? That was a shame mostly reserved for women.

"What are you talking about?"

I used my feet to scoot forward, rolling the bike closer and getting grim satisfaction at watching him try to merge with the tree. I didn't stop until my front tire pressed against him, drawing a pathetic whimper.

A part of me understood I shouldn't revel in his fear.

A more primal part loved it.

"I'm offended you don't remember. You're the fucker who held me down so his buddy could hurt me," I stated.

"I don't know who—" He tried to lie, and

my bike took offense, growling into Skinny's trembling body.

"I'm sorry!" he squeaked. "I didn't mean to. But when Joey gets an idea in his head, it's easier to just go along."

"Easier? Your friend Joey is a rapist," I hissed.

"But I'm not. And I'm doing my best to make better choices."

"Says the guy who is high right now."

"Because I'm weak. It's not my fault. It's the drugs." He bobbed his head as if that excused his behavior.

It didn't in my world. "Hurting innocent people is wrong." I pressed forward with the bike.

"You're hurting me," he whimpered.

"You're not innocent."

"Please," he blubbered, but it was the scent of piss that woke me from the madness.

What the fuck was I doing, terrorizing this man? Who gave me permission to punish him?

He did when he victimized me.

I ignored that voice to ask, "What's your name?"

"Sawyer."

"Sawyer what?" I snapped.

"Kyle Sawyer."

"Well, Kyle Sawyer, enjoy your last hour of freedom."

"What are you going to do?" he asked as I began to wheel away.

"Going to make sure you get the justice you deserve."

I'd call Brayden the moment I got home. Maybe he'd videotape the arrest for me. Give me closure.

Hopefully, this Sawyer fucker didn't try to leave town. Didn't matter. If necessary, I'd find him again. Don't ask me where the certainty came from.

Elation filled me for the whole ride home. Once I'd put the bike away in the garage for the night—after wiping it down and putting a blanket over it to protect it from dust—I went home. Blade barely lifted his head from the couch.

"Good thing I wasn't a burglar, huh?"

He farted in reply. Effective and might just scare off any wannabe thieves given the noxious smell.

I put my dog into the yard to do his business, and went to text Brayden, only to pause.

How should I explain where I'd gotten Kyle

Sawyer's name? Which led to a lightbulb I'm-so-dumb moment. Dammit, why didn't I ask Sawyer where to find his buddy, Joey?

Blame being so frazzled by power. Being in control empowered.

I gnawed my lower lip and stuck to a partial truth as I texted.

Hey, took the bike out for a short spin and came across some junkies under the bridge spanning the train tracks. Saw one of the guys who attacked me. Name of Kyle Sawyer in case you're bored and want to check it out. I re-read what I'd type so far and grimaced. So romantic. What could I add? *Or you could come over.*

Way too forward. I erased it.

I sighed and looked away for a second. My adrenaline faded fast, leaving me tired and lonely. As if he heard, Blade wandered to me by the back door and leaned against my leg.

Okay, so not fully alone, but my dog wasn't the same as having someone who could actually hold me and tell me everything would be okay. I typed a new message and hit send before I could change my mind.

Feeling a little shook and wouldn't mind some company.

The honest truth. I didn't exactly get what I wished for.

"How was the ride?" a deep voice drawled.

Mahoney was back.

CHAPTER 19

I BLAMED STRESS FOR MY SUDDEN HALLUCINATION because I knew for a fact that I hadn't fallen asleep.

"The ride was good. Great, actually." Liberating.

"Acceleration?"

"Decent, although I didn't push for the first run. I took the bike on an easy cruise."

Mahoney nodded in approval. "Cautious the first time is good. Wish I could have gone with you."

"Shame the motorcycle only seats one."

"We'd both fit if you got close and held on tight for the ride." Mahoney winked in an obvious flirt.

I wasn't about to play romantic games with

a figment of my imagination.

"I'm not crazy." A mantra I repeated aloud as I walked back into the house, ignoring the man who followed.

"Only crazy people talk to themselves," he remarked.

"No shit," I muttered, kicking off my shoes.

Mahoney remained by the back door and whistled. My dog came barreling inside, paws covered in mud.

"Sit!" I yelled and grabbed the towel meant for such an occasion. A cleaning wipe over the paws and then the floor involved me bent over, ass up in the air.

Mahoney whistled. "Talk about being cruel. Do you know how hard I'm having to resist slapping that thing?"

"Slap it and die."

"Worth it." *Crack.*

He slapped. I yelped and righted myself. "What are you doing?" And how could it feel so real? A hallucination didn't have the power to hurt. But then again, neither did a ghost.

A smug smirk creased his rugged features. "I cannot be held responsible. You asked for it."

"I did not ask you to hit me."

"Bah. Barely. I went easy on you."

"You will refrain from hitting me."

"That's not hitting. And let's get one thing clear, I don't beat on women."

"My throbbing cheek begs to differ." It did quiver, but not in pain. I'd enjoyed the tap, although I'd never admit it.

"Want me to kiss it better?"

I did. What did that say about me?

That I obviously needed to go to bed. Getting all horny because my imagination chose to subject me to chest-thumping alpha male misogynistic subjugation.

I kicked off my boots and tromped away from Mahoney to ready myself for bed. Knowing he didn't exist didn't make stripping in front of him easy. My fingers trembled as I undid the zipper and button for my jeans. I shoved my pants down. My T-shirt remained clean under my hoodie, so I just threw the red fabric onto the floor so I'd remember to wash it, and then took off the bra by undoing the clip and pulling off the straps through the armholes. My shirt never came off, and he noticed.

"Cheater. Or should I call you a tease?" he purred, and my nipples reacted, pushing noticeably at the fabric of my shirt.

I fled to the bathroom and brushed my teeth. Mahoney stood outside the door. Part of his reflection appeared on the edge of my mirror. Haunting me.

Yet he didn't frighten me. Oddly enough, I felt safe in his presence. Comforted by an imaginary protector. Obviously, my mind struggled with the trauma I'd experienced and fabricated his spectral presence to deal with it. Who would have thought being jumped would mess with my head so much? Apparently, I wasn't handling it as well as I'd thought.

"No nail polish?"

I glanced down at my bare toes. I'd not had a pedicure in ages. "Nope. Waste of time."

"Says you. What am I supposed to admire when they're up around my ears?"

"Mahoney!" I shouted in shock and realized it was the first time I'd used his name.

And, apparently, he didn't like it. "It's Junkdog."

"I am not calling you Junkdog."

His lips quirked. "Why not?"

"Because it's dumb." I remained blunt.

"Yeah. It is. I got it young and thought it was cool."

"You're not young anymore."

He rolled his shoulders. "And yet, it stuck. How about you call me Killian?"

"No offense, but given the accusations against you, you really should think of changing it."

"Anything else, babycakes?"

I winced. "Ew. What the fuck kind of name is that?"

"Don't you like it."

"No. My name is Allie, short for Alyssa."

"Too nice. If you're going to ride, you'll need something else. Maybe Fiery Vixen."

Me, a fiery vixen? I would dare any woman not to feel pleasure at the sensual way he gazed upon me. The smoldering interest. The way his hands actually felt as if they tugged my waist, drawing me close, the weight of them heavy. Claiming.

I glanced up at him. His gaze met mine. Then dropped to my lips. His head lowered for a kiss, and the strangest thought hit me. Did making out with the imaginary Mahoney count as masturbation?

Before his mouth connected, I shoved to give myself space. "Not happening."

As I walked away, Mahoney murmured, "It will."

CHAPTER 20

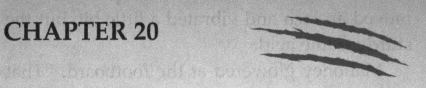

MAHONEY'S PROMISE GAVE ME TINGLES. HOW sexually bereft was I to be turned on by what amounted to my imagination?

As I pulled back my comforter, Mahoney said, "Who is Kyle Sawyer?"

"A lowlife." I eyed him suspiciously. "Where did you hear that name? Were you reading my private text messages?"

Rather than reply, he frowned. "This Kyle Sawyer scares you. Why?"

"He doesn't," I lied. The mention of him killed my desire, and I inwardly shook. Facing down my attacker, I'd been full of adrenaline. Now that it had worn off, a chill filled my limbs.

With a shiver, I crawled into my bed and

pulled up the covers. A second later, Blade skirted around Mahoney to bound onto the bed and squash me. The bed squeaked as it moved an inch and vibrated a little bit, but the sturdy frame held.

Mahoney glowered at the footboard. "That fucker hurt you."

"He did. Not as bad as his friend, Joey, though. Good thing your old bike fell on me the night they attacked. It might have literally saved my life."

"I remember you needing help." He frowned.

"No, you don't, because you weren't there." I'd been all alone then, and despite the figment talking to me, was alone now.

Rather than reply, Mahoney turned from me. "Are you still seeing that detective?"

"Brayden? Yes. He's just been really busy with work. There's a serial killer in town, using the same three blades as in a previous set of murders." I stared hard at him.

A snorting noise erupted. "You're still convinced it's me when you should be worried about the fact that if it's not, then who is it? And are you next?"

My lips flattened. "Don't bother trying to

scare me. It's unlikely I'm in danger since I don't fit the profile.

"And what's this supposed profile?"

"Ten years ago, the killer went after scum. Folks no one cared about because they were foul. One of the newer cases involved a cop."

"Maybe it was a bad cop."

"Maybe." My mind mulled over the two old cases that didn't jibe with any of the rest. Why had those two seemingly innocent people died in the initial murder spree? Did they have a secret life nobody had caught on to?

"Worried about that cop you're dating?"

My lips pursed. "I don't know if I'd call it dating." I settled deeper into my pillow, and he joined me, sitting on the mattress, stretching out around Blade and me, causing the whole bed to creak. My imagination worked overtime.

"Be careful."

I hugged my dog and buried my nose in his fur. "I'll be fine. If anyone comes after me, Blade will save me."

He didn't laugh but he did turn somber as he said, "I won't let anyone hurt you."

If he were real, I would have jumped him. I might be strong and independent, but it would have been nice to have someone who cared in my corner. But Mahoney didn't exist. Despite knowing I spoke to myself, I asked, "Does the name Valerie Loome ring any bells?" She was one of the innocents who'd died in the serial killing ten years ago.

He stiffened.

"You know her!" An accusation that turned his lips down.

"Yeah, I know her. We used to date while in the gang."

I blinked as the missing piece filled in. "She was a member of the Trikillz?"

"Yeah, we both joined young, but she left in her mid-teens. Val's mom took her out of state to some small town and got her clean."

"And Barry Nugent?" I threw the other name at him, and he frowned.

"Nah. Don't know no Barry."

There went that theory.

"Unless…" he mused aloud.

"What?"

"Used to run with a guy called Nugget."

"Scar over his right brow?" I queried to be certain.

"Left, actually. And he wore a hoop dangling a cross in his ear. And why are you asking?"

"The Triclaw Killer murdered them," I stated.

His lip curled. "No, that was the gang. Because they didn't get permission to leave."

"You did."

"Aye, but it cost me. And in the end, it didn't matter. Despite me turning over a new leaf, the cops had it out for me." His lips twisted.

"Do you know who's killing people now?"

"Does it matter? I hear they're cleaning up the streets."

"They murdered a cop."

"Under investigation for dealing drugs stolen from lockup. Not exactly a nice guy."

"He was also one of the cops trying to arrest you way back when. Coincidence?"

"Not really. All the dicks on my case were crooked. They should all die." The vehemence in the statement gave me a chill.

I had to warn Brayden. Of what, exactly, I couldn't say. I only knew that he deserved to know that he might be in danger.

"I need to send a message," I muttered, reaching for my phone.

Mahoney knocked it from my hand. "It's late."

"And? Even if he's sleeping, he'll see it in the morning."

"He who?" Mahoney rumbled, acting all macho.

"My boyfriend." I popped the hard syllables.

"Not your boyfriend. You said it yourself not so long ago. Not to mention, he still hasn't fucked you."

"I'll have you know he fucked me hard."

"Liar."

"He's an accomplished lover." I dug myself in deeper.

"Now, you're really piling on the bullshit." He dragged me against him.

"What are you doing?"

"I gave your loser detective a chance to claim you. Now, it's my turn."

Alpha-male logic at its finest. It shouldn't have titillated. Was this what my subconscious thought I wanted? "Excuse me, but that's not up to you. I decide who I sleep with."

"We'll fuck," he stated with assurance. "And once we do, I'll ruin you for anyone else."

"Hate to break it to you," I whispered, "but I'll always take sex with a real guy over that of a ghost."

"I'm not a ghost," he hotly retorted.

"What year is it?"

"I don't see what—"

"It's not a hard question. What year is it? Which team won last year's football championship? Or would you be more familiar with hockey?"

"Argh, why must you be so difficult?" he bellowed and shot straight up through my bedroom ceiling.

Freaky, and the following roar that shook my house was kind of sexy because that was the cry of a man in the thralls of sexual frustration. Even if I imagined the whole thing, I enjoyed it.

I slept like my dog after shaking for a full day because of five minutes of audible fireworks. That was to say soundly, probably snoring loudly and definitely drooling on my pillow. Until the doorbell woke me.

I rolled and groaned. "Go away." I wanted to snuggle my pillow longer. It was much too early to get up.

Ding. Dong.

Only as I blinked open an eyelid did I realize that I'd slept past dawn. Shit, I'd gotten a full night's sleep, and if my clock could be believed, hit the unbelievable hour of 7:07 a.m.

The pounding at my front door roused my dog's head. He cracked his jaw, yawning, his expression not happy at being disturbed.

"I agree," I muttered. "Someone needs to cool their jets."

"Allie! Are you in there?"

Hearing Brayden's voice perked me up immensely. I rolled out of bed to find myself in only panties. What the fuck? I'd thought I'd gone to bed in a T-shirt. Must have had a hot flash in the middle of the night and stripped. In good news, I'd forgotten to put in a pad but appeared to be crimson-tide-free!

Bang. Bang.

"Hold on a second," I hollered. Where had I put my shirt? Pants? As I fished around for clothing, I caught a peek of red in the closet. Opening it revealed my red sweater shoved to the side on the floor. I didn't remember kicking it in there. Nor the dark stain on it.

Bang, rattle. "Allie, I need you to answer."

"Coming!" Someone appeared rather impatient. Maybe he finally had more than twenty minutes to hang out for once. I forwent a hair-brush but snared a piece of gum to chomp on my way to the door. The college toothbrush of champions.

Hoping my hair didn't appear as if rats had abandoned it looking for upgraded digs, I opened the door and offered my most winsome smile. "Hey, handsome."

My greeting did not erase the scowl from Brayden's face. "Can I come in?"

"Well, duh. Of course, you can." I stepped aside. "What's up? You look like someone pissed in your last bowl of cereal."

"Listen, Allie, this isn't actually a social call. I need to ask you some questions."

"About?"

"Where were you last night?"

"In bed. Alone because you were busy." Yup, I blamed him for that. If he'd come by like I'd texted, I wouldn't have had to flirt with the fake Mahoney.

"I'm being serious."

"So am I. Where else would I be?"

"Riding a certain motorcycle."

"Oh, yeah. I got the bike going and took her for a small spin."

"You shouldn't have done that."

"Look at you, Mr. Rules all of a sudden. I know, I should have waited to get a plate and a helmet, but I couldn't resist. I didn't go far, and nothing happened."

"You call confronting one of your assailants nothing?"

"How...?" Rather than keep asking, I lifted my chin. I wasn't going to deny anything. "Yeah, I did run into one of my attackers. And I'm sorry, but the second I saw him, I snapped."

"What were you thinking?" he yelled.

A part of me understood that he worried. Another part did not like his tone.

My hand hit my hip, his only warning before I laid into him. "Don't you fucking yell at me unless it's to say thank you. After all, unlike you, I managed to at least get the name of the guy who attacked me."

His lips turned down. "Have you told anyone else about running into your assailant? Then again, I'm not sure if it matters given the witnesses."

A frown creased my brow. "You're not making sense."

"People saw what you did, Allie."

I confronted my abuser. How dare he act as

if I were in the wrong? "So what if I confronted Sawyer? He deserved it. Every last bit."

Brayden gaped at me. "I can't believe you said that."

"Seriously? I can't believe you don't think he deserved it. The guy held me down for his buddy to rape. I think I'm perfectly entitled to curse him out. And I won't apologize for scaring him so bad he pissed his pants. That's not a crime."

"No, but killing him is."

CHAPTER 21

It took me a second to filter what Brayden HAD said. "Hold your fucking mustangs. Are you saying Kyle Sawyer is dead?"

"We're still waiting on confirmation of his identity since none was found on the body."

"Then it might not be him."

"Those same eyewitnesses that saw you accost him have confirmed it's Sawyer."

I didn't like the way he said that. "How did he die?"

"As if you don't know." He gave a slight shake of his head.

"Is this a trick question? Because I didn't kill him. Last I saw the skinny fucker, he was blubbering and snotting and smelling of pee."

"Now he's in a morgue with his belly slashed open."

I cut straight to the chase. "How many wounds?"

He glared at me. "Three, which you well know."

My temper flared. "No, I don't. Because I had nothing to do with it." But I would shake the hand of the person who did because that fucker didn't deserve to live.

"As if you'd admit it," he muttered.

Where did this accusation come from? Incredulity had me asking, "Do I seriously look like a killer?"

"No. And I thought the Allie I'd gotten to know would never do such a thing, but then I talked to someone who was there. She says you terrorized him."

"Holy fuck. I called him a few names. It's not my fault he has a weak bladder. I didn't leave a single mark. Unlike what he and Joey did to me. Funny how that works. I end up beaten and in a hospital, and yet I'm the one being harassed."

"I realize this is uncomfortable, but I have to ask these questions because a man has been found murdered, and you have motive."

"To hate, yes. Not to kill." I wouldn't have thought that merited saying aloud.

"I want to believe you, Allie. Promise me you didn't do it." He dragged me against his body and searched my face. "Swear to me."

"I shouldn't have to because you should know me better by now," I huffed. The easier thing would have been to swear to him. Me, a killer? Preposterous. Yet, I couldn't help but recollect those blank spots in my memory. The blackouts where I started in one place and woke up somewhere else.

He grabbed my hands and squeezed them too hard. "If I'm crazy, it's because of you. You distract me from my work. When I'm around you, I can't think straight." His impassioned speech ended with him dragging me close and kissing me hard.

Oh, hell no. I bit him.

"Ouch." He recoiled and put fingers to his abused lip. "Why did you do that?"

No remorse on my part. "You don't get to kiss me after accusing me of murder."

"I had no choice but to ask."

"Because you're a cop. I get it. I thought I was your girlfriend, though."

"You are."

"No, apparently, I'm not. But the fact that we were involved, along with new developments, is a strong indicator that you should be recusing yourself from the investigation in the Triclaw Murders."

"I should. But I won't." He shrugged and didn't look the least bit apologetic.

"Why not?"

"Because it will be easier to keep you out of jail if I'm involved."

I gaped and ripped my hands free from his, giving him a shove. "You think I did it."

"Not intentionally. You probably only meant to blow off some steam and it got out of hand. I get it. Things happen in the heat of the moment." Look at him being so understanding.

Except...

"I didn't kill anyone!" I shrieked.

"Have to admit it was clever, using the same method on Sawyer as the Triclaw Killer. The task force probably won't bother looking elsewhere for a suspect. In good news, the crime scene appeared clean. It was smart thinking to give yourself an alibi by texting me and inviting me over. If anyone asks, tell them we spent the night together."

He truly thought I'd done it.

Un-fucking-believable.

"Out." I shoved him in the direction of the door.

"Why are you mad? I'm on your side, Allie."

He sounded sincere, yet I'd seen the shows that depicted the po-po and their deception. Could be he lied to draw me into admitting something. He'd pull out a hidden microphone, distort my words, and off I'd go to jail.

No way.

Because I was like ninety percent sure I had nothing to do with Sawyer's death.

As for the last ten percent... I wanted to replay my security camera footage to be sure. First, though, I needed to be alone.

Of course, after days of me wanting him to stay, and him being unable, the one time I wanted him to make a swift departure, Brayden wouldn't leave easily. "I looked into Mahoney's sister."

I paused long enough to ask, "And what did you find?"

"He had one called Gwendolyn."

Which could easily be shortened to Ginny. "Did you talk to her?"

He shook his head. "Can't. She's dead. Died a year before Mahoney disappeared."

"How?" I asked, seeing his expression.

"Three slashes to her stomach."

"That's terrible." My hand hit my mouth to cover my gasp.

"A gang hit from the looks of it. Guessing since they couldn't get at Mahoney, they sent a message through his sister."

"You said it happened a year before he disappeared."

"His sister died a few days before the first murder." Brayden remarked, and a light bulb went off in my head.

"He went after his old gang for revenge." Even managed to find a way to get the ones in prison. It made sense, even as my mind fought the truth. It wanted to cling to my romanticized version of Mahoney as the reformed bad guy. In truth, the real Mahoney was a murdering thug. Still, I wasn't about to tell Brayden that. "Sounds like he did the cops a favor by taking out the trash."

"He's a killer." Brayden spat.

"Was. Mahoney is dead, you said so yourself."

"Is he?"

Because his serious mien freaked me out, I quipped, "Maybe it's his ghost." The ludicrous suggestion slipped from my lips before I could stop it.

Brayden froze and stared at me for a good long moment before saying, "You got something you want to tell me, Allie?"

Admit that I was interacting with a figment of my mind?

Nope.

"I'm done talking for the moment. You and your case can go snuggle somewhere else." My annoyance with him remained.

Accusing me of murder.

Ha!

More like his hatred of Mahoney clouded his view. Apparently, me owning the same property and rebuilding Junkdog's bike had him conflating me with his nemesis.

Finally, it hit Brayden that he'd gone too far. "Don't be mad. I only want to protect you."

"You have a funny way of showing it." I opened the door and pointed. "Good day, Detective."

"Don't be like that. Are you crabby because you're still on your period?"

I arched a brow. "I am going to pretend you didn't just say that. Go."

He sighed. "You know how to get in touch with me."

Yes, but I wouldn't. I didn't plan to be the kind of weak woman who needed a man in her life. Even if it was a hot detective. I refused to date a man who thought me capable of murder. I slammed the door shut and locked it for good measure.

"Glad now we never slept together," I murmured as I headed to the living room and the only male I needed for true happiness.

My dog.

"What do you say I make a whole package of bacon for breakfast?"

Blade agreed wholeheartedly.

CHAPTER 22

WHILE THE BACON FRIED, I PROPPED MY TABLET on the counter to check out what was being said online about Sawyer's murder.

The news websites had the bare facts, mostly pertaining to my assailant. Accused of assault and robbery and in and out of jails since he turned eighteen. The article stated Sawyer had been found dead of apparent stab wounds. A kinder way of saying he'd been gutted.

They went on to claim they suspected it was drug-related. No mention of me. Could it be Brayden had kept my name out of the mix? How, though, if witnesses claimed to have seen me? Or at least seen a woman. I'd never taken off my goggles or hood.

The bacon crisped, and I threw some on a paper towel to degrease it for me but left the rest in the pan for my dog. I dumped in some dry food. I know, not the healthiest thing, but it did wonders for his coat. I'd take sleek over frizzy and dander-shedding any day.

As I indulged in my breakfast of champions, that featured eggnog snared at the grocery store since Thanksgiving neared, and dried banana chips because the real thing tended to rot forgotten, I flicked through a few more articles all stating the same thing. Basically, the piece of shit got what he deserved.

Munching on bacon wrapped around a banana chip—don't knock it 'til you've tried it—I hit social media for my entertainment—someone's animal doing something cute, people being assholes to each other, every minutia of life caught on film for those who wanted to watch and mock...because, let's be honest, other people's misery gave us that rush we didn't want to admit: that sense that we were better than someone.

Deny it. Go ahead. We both know that pretending you don't feel such a base emotion feeds your always hungry sense of self-righteousness.

The meaningless images flowed past

without drawing my attention. I changed to another social media channel, and the hashtag #redhood and #steelwolf immediately caught my attention, especially since they appeared to be trending in the Ottawa Valley.

I clicked and gaped at the post someone named Poke-Me-Sally shared. Apparently, Sally had been one of the tweakers gathered around the barrel last night. She'd typed out a vivid and imaginative story about my encounter with Sawyer. I read with a brow lifted in disbelief.

...she came barreling out of nowhere, riding this big black wolf with blazing red eyes. The color of rubies and blood, just like her cloak. I never saw her face on account the hood covered her head, but I seen inside enough to realize she wasn't human with those black, bottomless pits for eyes.

The more I read, the more my jaw dropped. I finished with a disbelieving snort.

...as the Red Hood raced off, she cried out, "The night is mine." Then disappeared on her steel wolf. But she'll be back now that she's had a taste of blood. Tainted blood being her favorite. Which is why this is day one of sobriety. I have to stay clean to live.

Sally had added a blurry image of what

might have been me on the bike if someone had added a Hell filter. Like, seriously, the whole thing emerged as a swirl of reds and oranges streaked with shadows. The flames in the barrel, a portal to Hell. My bike's headlights shone with a fire I didn't recall, illuminating the man being threatened.

Sawyer—or so I assumed by the smudge that might be a face.

The good news? No one—other than Brayden—would ever associate that person in the picture with me. Just like no one in their right mind would believe that overwrought crap Sally had written. Only it turned out a segment of the population wanted to.

The original post got shared so many times, the comment section exploded. By that afternoon, Sally's friend had added an artistic rendition of me. A much sexier version where my buxom frame wore leather that served no practical purpose, and a cloak that would get caught in my wheels if I ever dared to ride with it. Preposterous. Yet I saved a copy of it because...hello, I kind of wanted to be that kickass chick on the wolf bike, red cloak streaming behind me as I raced towards a tattooed and evil-looking dude. Imagine me as a crime-fighting babe.

I probably should have been worried all these random strangers thought that I'd killed not only Sawyer but also the cop and some other dude wanted on rape charges. At the same time, and to my intense disbelief, they applauded my actions. They saw me as a vigilante out to make the world a better place. It appeared that those who'd died had left behind more enemies than friends.

And I had a fan club. One I would never encourage. I'd seen how quickly a wave of support could turn. How easy it would be for them to suddenly transform me into the villain of this piece. The news did it all the time, taking the victim and painting them as the aggressor while the real criminal walked on a technicality.

Fear of being recognized led to me being hesitant about going out on the bike. I should lay low. Tell that to the wild energy coursing through my veins that had me pacing my living room.

I have to get out. I'd go stir crazy otherwise.

If I ran errands in my car, no one would ever connect me to the Red Hood or the Steel

Wolf. My nice, dependable vehicle would be a better choice for picking up supplies to start work on my next wreck.

Rather than being responsible, and without conscious knowledge of how it'd happened, I found myself riding the Steel Wolf, laughing at the wind buffeting my bare cheeks.

I pulled over instantly and jumped off the bike.

How had I gotten here?

I blinked at the road, Highway 7. Almost home. No helmet on my head, but during this blackout, I'd apparently invested in better goggles. I pulled them off to admire the tinted glass and the cool, steampunk style. The padding around the eyepieces and strap meant they fit much more snugly and comfortably. I vaguely remembered trying them on and making faces in a mirror.

After the glasses I went looking for...

The blank spot faded as I recalled the latter part of my afternoon. The leather store, which explained my new jacket. The dark crimson of it smooth to the touch.

My gaze went to the package strapped to the tank. I remembered what was in that folded bag.

My cheeks heated.

What was I thinking when I'd bought that leather outfit? Impractical, overpriced, and totally not me. Yet I'd slapped it on the counter and paid too much. The thing was fucking hot, and I wanted to feel sexy. The question being, would I have the guts to model it? And if I did, who would I show it to?

Calmed, I got back on my bike and finished my ride home, letting her rip and reveling in the power between my legs. My happiness soured at the sight of Brayden leaning against his car in my driveway, face bearing a deep scowl. My bike hummed to a stop, and my booted foot engaged the stand as I swung off.

"Where have you been?" Brayden demanded as if I owed him answers.

"Out." I removed the new tinted goggles before pulling off my scrunchie and shaking out my hair.

"You should wear a helmet."

I didn't appreciate his tone. "I think I might just pay the ticket for riding without one and live on the wild side."

"A wild side that will end the first time you pitch headfirst over those handlebars and smash your head."

A good point. Maybe I'd wear a beanie style so I could keep the glasses. "I don't need you telling me what to do."

"Apparently, you do. How could you be so stupid?" Brayden didn't try to make up with me, he went on a rant. "You went out in public on *that* bike after what happened last night? Are you trying to get caught?"

"No one recognized me," I muttered as I unstrapped the packages on the back, a splurge that I doubted the detective would appreciate. I hugged the bundle to my chest as I headed for the house.

"Allie..." His tone cajoled, but I snapped.

"Don't *Allie* me. Last time you were here, you called me a murderer." And, apparently, he'd not returned to apologize.

"I said if you were, I'd help you conceal the fact, given you had reason."

"That's not any better." I rolled my eyes.

"It's the best I can do given the mounting evidence against you."

"What evidence? People saw someone talking to Sawyer. That's it. I left him alive."

"And returned when no one could see you to finish him off."

"Conjecture."

"It's circumstantial enough. Especially given your connection to the murdering Mahoney."

Exasperation had me huffing, "Oh, for fuck's sake. This has nothing to do with Mahoney. He's gone. Dead or vanished. Doesn't really matter since I have nothing to do with him."

"You took over his property, which is a link."

"If you think that's evidence, you need to go back to detective school. People buy properties involved in crime all the time, doesn't make them criminals."

"You also rebuilt his motorcycle, and given the resurgence of Triclaw Murders, I can almost wager a member of the task force has suggested you're a groupie reenacting his crimes."

"A groupie for a serial killer?" Now was not the time to admit my horny dreams about Mahoney.

"It's actually quite common."

"I didn't even know he existed when I bought this place!"

"Is that the truth, or are you sticking to a story to appear innocent?"

"I *am* innocent!" I shouted. Even if I weren't, how dare he assume I had anything to do with anyone's murder?

"Let's say you are innocent—"

"Because I am," I muttered darkly.

"—that means someone's out there killing people."

"Don't they have any leads?"

"Nope, because I've kept them away from the only one." He stared at me as he said it.

The theatrics had me clapping. I'll admit to being impressed that his imagination could be as vivid as mine. "Bravo. That's quite the fabrication. I'm beginning to think you just come around to throw a scare into me. It's not going to work. I am not admitting to anything because there's nothing to admit. Like there is nothing to link me to those dead cops."

"Mahoney." He had one simple, repetitive reply.

I rolled my eyes at his insistence. "Mahoney's gone."

"The man, yes. But what of his spirit?" He dropped it out there all casual-like.

"Oh, hell no. Not this again. A ghost can't be a murderer." He was insane for even suggesting it.

EVE LANGLAIS

"It's not crazy because it's true. I know you've seen him." A sharp statement. "Don't deny it."

"And if I said yes?" Could I finally admit that maybe, just *maybe*, the Mahoney I knew was more than a figment of my mind? What if it *was* his spirit?

"If he's returned, then you are in grave danger." I could see that he believed it.

I, however, wasn't playing into his sick fantasy. "I'm fucking with you, Brayden. I haven't seen a ghost. I can't because they're not real." Much as I wanted to use that excuse for my Mahoney hallucinations, I retained enough wits to recognize true versus false.

"Ghosts, spirits, remnants. They exist."

"So, you've met some?"

"No, but the evidence is there for their existence if you look."

"And so what if they do?"

"Some possess a strength of will that can leave behind a strong residue when they die."

"That does what? Can't see one doing much damage without a body." I had to wonder why I argued his theory. After all, I'd rather he blame a ghost than me for the killing of people.

"Sometimes insidious whispers are

worse." The ardent expression let me know he believed every word spewing from his mouth.

"Ghosts aren't real. They're hysterical expressions of an overwrought mind." A fancy phrase I'd read somewhere on the internet, give or take a few big words.

"I can see you don't want to believe me. You're not ready yet to admit the world has mysteries we can't always comprehend. But, one day, you'll see. And you'll want my aid. Call me when you do. Especially if Mahoney's spirit appears to you. He's dangerous, but I know how we can get rid of him." His intent desire to help me shone through his crazy statements.

Perhaps he'd seen too much in his police career, and his mind had snapped. Whatever the case, it didn't matter. "I won't be calling you. Ever, Brayden."

"I'm trying to help you. I care about you." When he reached for me, I stepped away.

"No." While still attractive with looks that fired my blood, I'd lost my passion for the man.

"Allie," he murmured softly. "I know this is a lot to take in. I've so much to tell you."

"I'm not interested in any of your delu-
sional fantasies."

"Don't be mad. "

Mad? No. More like disappointed that he'd
turned out not as expected. "You should go."

"I'd rather stay here with you."

Truth. I could feel it in the way he grabbed
my hands so that he might move in close. He
pressed hard against my lower belly, and I felt
an answering tingle. No period this time to get
in our way. Nothing but me.

"I think I need a bit of time to think about
this. Us..." It was one thing to snicker at
memes that claimed the best kind of lover or
friend wouldn't ask why you needed to bury a
body but where to bring the shovel. It proved
another thing to have a guy thinking that you
were capable of murder and then offering to
cover it up.

Romantic or a sign of something else?

"As you wish." He didn't push me and left.

I hated him a little for it.

CHAPTER 23

I LEFT THE BIKE PARKED IN MY DRIVEWAY AND went into the house, still carrying my purchase. I tossed it onto the kitchen table with a grimace. So much for my giddy high of earlier. Buying the risqué outfit had brought back that feeling of the time I'd smuggled home my first thong, knowing if Mom found it, she'd call me a whore.

In retrospect, I couldn't say what'd compelled me to buy the revealing ensemble until I heard a bag crinkle and Mahoney say, "Nice outfit. When are you going to model it for me?"

I cast him a coquettish grin as he dangled it in front of me. "Who says it's for you?" Yes, I flirted with my hallucination.

"You're dating a cop. Doubt he's into the biker-chick look."

"I don't know. And I doubt I ever will." My lips turned down.

"Trouble in paradise? Let me guess, still no sex."

I grimaced. "No sex, but now, it's by choice. The man thinks I murdered someone."

"Cool."

"Cool?" I whirled. "What is it with people thinking I can kill?"

"Would you prefer I said I doubted you were capable? Because if I did, I'm pretty sure you'd suddenly get all feminist on me and blah blah blah about how you're just as capable as a man."

"Wow, all that misogyny in one sentence. Where do I start?"

"See, this is why I hate talking to women. As far as I'm concerned, your lips are best suited for other things." His gaze dropped to his groin.

"As if I'd ever blow you." Hotly exclaimed.

"You would and you'd enjoy it."

"Shows how much you know." I'd never been big on giving head. Although the reverse wasn't true. Loved it when people went down on me.

"So, this cop you're dating, Brody—"

"Brayden," I corrected.

"How come I've never seen him around?"

"Because you always seem to disappear when he visits. Funny how that works." A real poltergeist with the hots for me would have stayed to haunt his ass.

"You like this guy?"

"I thought I did." I shrugged. "Now, I don't know. I mean, he's still hot and all, and I wish I'd jumped his bones when I had the chance. Now, the more he tries to be nice, the more—I don't know—I'm turned off, I guess." Apparently, all those magazines and cheesy surveys were right. Women preferred the bad boys. In my case, an imaginary, dead one.

"If you're feeling neglected…" He leered in a way that tempted me.

Instead, I sighed. "I should go to bed."

"So early?" His left brow arched.

"Given I'm hallucinating, it's probably for the best." I really should talk to a doctor about my Mahoney problem. Could be a brain tumor causing the issue. Or seeping gases from underneath the junkyard.

Lying in bed didn't shut him up. Worse, Mahoney lay on the bed beside me. "What if you're not imagining things?"

"You're not real." I put an arm over my eyes and tried not to shiver as he ran a finger over the bare flesh.

"Are you sure?"

"I'm the only one who sees you."

"Because you're obviously special, baby-cakes. Did you ever think maybe I don't want to talk to anyone else?"

"Hold on." I moved my arm to eye him. "Are you finally admitting that you're not real?"

"I'm real to you. Real to me. But the rest of the world…" He frowned. "I feel as if there's something missing. The reason *why* and how I ended up caught between the living world and wherever it is I find myself."

"Limbo?"

"I guess that's possible."

"You talk as if you're dead."

His lips twisted. "It would explain the holes in my memory."

"What do you remember?"

"This place. The bike." He rolled to his back and tucked a hand under his head.

"Don't forget your sister."

"Yeah. Ginny." Sadness tugged his features down. "She must have been so upset when I stopped coming around."

"It's not your fault." Look at me soothing the ghost of an accused serial killer. I didn't tell him that Ginny had died before he disappeared. He seemed upset enough.

His lips twisted. "It's because I chose the wrong path in life. And it cost me my life."

"What makes you say that?"

"Because no fucking way would I ever leave Ginny."

"Let's say you *were* killed. Where's your body?" I'd gone past the point of caring if I imagined him or if his spirit chose to speak to me. It felt too real to ignore.

"Fuck if I know."

But I wondered. Ghosts usually haunted the areas of their death. If spirit Mahoney truly existed, it seemed to indicate that his body remained nearby.

Where? I couldn't really see it in the tiny yard of the house. More likely, he'd be dumped in the junkyard. Stuff him in a trunk and bury him under trash. Given the mess out here, his bones might remain undetected for a long time. After all, how many mountains of junk did I have to sort?

He rolled and hugged me against him. "Fuck talking. We should be fucking."

I snorted. "Aren't you romantic?" Then, because my lie of omission tickled my guilt, I found myself whispering, "Ginny died a year before you disappeared."

He stiffened. "What? No. How?"

"Reports called it a Trikillz gang hit."

He exhaled loudly for a ghost. "She died almost instantly, according to the doc who did the autopsy—as if that was supposed to help. I almost fucking killed him for saying it.. I was so angry."

"You remember?"

"I wish I didn't." A soft admission.

"Did you kill your old gang in revenge?"

"Maybe. Probably. That time after Ginny's death is hazy."

"They deserved it for what they did."

My defense brought a rumbling chuckle. "Don't try and soothe my conscience, babycakes. I don't feel one bit guilty. Anyone who'd hurt my sweet little sister deserved whatever they got. And it probably explains why I'm dead." Meaning, he thought they'd taken him out.

He nuzzled and held me, not pressuring to do anything else. Not even a subtle grope.

With Blade crushing my feet at the end of the bed, I fell asleep in Mahoney's arms. He might not have a solid body in reality, but he kept me warm until I woke suddenly, mouth open on a scream. Clammy skin. Panting breaths. I struggled to stem my panic as a nightmare fled me in all its bloody gory.

What had I dreamt?

I lost it. And now that I'd truly woken, I realized that Mahoney was gone, but Blade had taken his place and breathed in my face. I shoved him away from me as I struggled to fight the fatigue pulling me down.

I stumbled into the bathroom to admire my bloodshot eyes. It looked as if I'd had little sleep, yet I'd been in bed by nine, and it was almost seven now. Why was I so tired? I kept getting full nights of undisturbed rest. Or so I assumed. Could I be sleepwalking? I'd check the video feeds to find out.

I ate cereal alongside my pooch as I perused the news online. Caught a live broadcast that froze my dripping milk and cereal spoon as the announcer claimed, "Another body was found last night, and sources close to the case claim it appears to be the work of a vigilante the people are calling Red Hood. For those not familiar with the latest online sensation…" The reporter gave a brief synopsis and even showed the anime cartoon version of me. Off by about twenty-five years, at least two cup sizes, and lips that looked painful. Add in the goggles and the fact that they'd given me really long, raven-black hair, and I remained anonymously safe.

Back to the latest victim. Apparently, someone had claimed they'd seen Red Hood and her wolfish bike just before the screaming had started by one Joseph Pescani. They flashed his mugshot, and I gasped.

It was him. Joey. My other attacker.

Dead by disembowelment.

My hand went to my lips. *No.*

It couldn't be me. I would never do something so heinous. But I recalled all that joking talk of Stephen King's horror classic and, suddenly, I wondered about the bike.

I raced from the house to the driveway. The bike I'd parked there the day before was gone.

Stolen? I should make sure. I flew through

the gate, headed for the garage, and entered to find the motorcycle. Uncovered. Leaning on its kickstand.

I perused it tip to tail. I didn't know what I expected to find. Bits of flesh, maybe some dried blood. The bike appeared clean and un-marred but for one difference. The tip of the front fender, ending in three raking strips, now shone a ruddy red. I ran my fingers over the smooth, new color and shuddered. I couldn't have said how or when it'd happened. The taint appeared to be part of the alloy.

My imagination ran wild with possibilities that all ended in one conclusion.

My bike's alive and killed those two druggies! Possibly even the cops.

Not the worst thing in the world, except for the fact that I owned the bike. If anyone traced the murders back to it, it would lead right to me. No one would ever believe that a hunk of metal was the real murderer.

"It's not the bike doing it." Mahoney spoke from behind me, and I whirled.

"Because it's you." I shoved at his chest. "Brayden was right. You're a killer."

"Am I? Deflect much?"

"Are you implying *I* had something to do

with it? Because I didn't." I pulled out my phone and showed him the screen. "The only motion alerts are from me just now. Nothing overnight."

He leaned close. "Nothing? Then explain how the bike got from the house to here."

I couldn't. Rather than reply, I fled the garage and locked it. Would that keep my possessed bike from joyriding for a new victim? A locked door certainly didn't stop Mahoney.

He stepped through, and I backed away. "Leave me alone."

"Would you calm the fuck down while I explain what's happening."

"Explain what? I thought you couldn't remember?"

"It's coming back to me slowly."

"Let me guess, if you kill more people, you might get all your memories back?" A hysterical exaggeration on my part, only he appeared pensive.

"It's certainly possible. After all—" He abruptly stopped talking and turned his head. "We have company."

Nice use of *we*, considering he disappeared. The gates rattled, and someone shouted, "Anyone in there?"

I shouted back. "Hold your horses. I'm coming."

Now, more than ever, I needed to not rock any boats and appear normal as a business. A great attitude to take until I saw who stood outside my gates.

The po-po had come for me.

CHAPTER 24

A PAIR OF POLICE OFFICERS IN DARK UNIFORMS waited beyond my locked gate. It took me a moment, due to trembling hands, to undo the lock. "What can I do for you, officers?"

"Are you Ms. Collins?"

"Yes. Can I ask what this is about?" I did my best not to let my nerves show. I clasped my hands and tried to project calm. Inside, I was screaming. Had they come to arrest me?

"Do you recognize this?" The officer with the thick mustache held up an evidence bag, holding a keychain I used to keep in my office. All kinds of keys, none that fit anything I'd found—yet—but I didn't want to toss them in case I eventually stumbled upon the stash.

"That keyring was stolen from me a few weeks ago during a robbery. Where did you find it?" As to how they knew it belonged to me? It held a metal tag with the junkyard address on it.

The officers glanced at each other before the female said, "It was located on the body of a deceased male."

I slapped my hand over my lips and did my utmost to look appropriately horrified. "Oh, no. What happened?"

"What usually happens to folks who live the high life," the male officer informed me somberly.

"Can I ask how he died?" I couldn't help but question. Let's be honest, most people in my position would have. Humanity lived for salacious details.

"A drug dispute turned fatal. Happens a lot among those kinds of people."

I heard the weariness in his tone. As a society, we tended to only see a fraction of the bad in the world. Cops, though, they dealt with it every single day.

"I guess he won't be hurting anyone else then." Perhaps a little tarter than the situation warranted, but I refused to feel sorry for that fucker, Joey. The world would be better off without him.

"No, he certainly won't be causing problems no more. On another note, sorry if no one's come by yet to take your statement. Staffing cuts have made it difficult for us to deal with the small crimes."

"I'd hardly call a hospitalization for my beating *small*."

"I agree. But, well, the higher-ups, they don't want us wasting time on druggie-related offenses because it never goes nowhere and just clogs up the courts."

"Because of the revolving door. Yeah, I get it." Why investigate a crime and go through the effort if the system would only release the perp, claiming mental health and addiction? I did almost mention that Brayden had been working my case, only to suddenly wonder… Maybe he wasn't supposed to be. From the start, his interest in me had seemed odd. A detective assigned to a robbery? And from the OPP, which usually dealt in provincial matters, not local affairs. That was usually the Ottawa police.

If Brayden were doing his own thing, then saying something might get him into trouble.

What if I changed my mind and decided to date him again? Perhaps I'd been too harsh. After all, the man wanted to help me cover up a murder. He obviously liked me a lot. But I had to wonder about some of the stuff he'd claimed.

These cops didn't act as if I were a murder suspect. Could be they acted a part, maybe hoping I'd inadvertently reveal something during their casual conversation about the dead guy. They could try all they liked; I knew nothing.

"Thank you for bringing me the news and the keys." I held out my hand, but the cop shook his head.

"Sorry, we gotta hold on to them until we know for sure they won't be needed."

"I thought it was an open-and-shut case." I acted innocent.

"Just crossing all the Ts and dotting the Is, ma'am."

I wanted to grimace at the *ma'am*; however, I'd reached an age where miss did not apply.

"Oh, that's fine. It's not like I need them." I offered a false smile.

"Did you want us to take your statement now about the robbery and assault?"

"Seems kind of pointless with my assailants dead."

Too late, I realized my slipup. By admitting that both of my attackers were dead, I'd given them a link to two bodies. Yikes.

Before the cops could pounce, the walkie at the woman's waist went off with a crackle. She and some crackly voice tossed off some numbers that ended with the woman jerking her head. "We got a call over in Carp we gotta run to."

The fellow tucked his thumbs in his belt loops. "We have to go."

"Sure. Yes, important things to do. Fighting crime and all that. Best of luck." I laid it on too thick in my nervousness.

"Feel free to pop by the station if you want to submit a report."

Like fuck would I waste my time on that.

The cops left, and I cursed Mahoney and that damned bike. Somehow, I just knew they were to blame.

Despite it only being midday on a Friday, I closed the gates and locked them. I didn't want to be disturbed.

I returned to my house and moped with my dog. Well, *I* moped, he napped on the couch, meaning I had to sit on the floor since I refused to be crushed under his body.

How had my life become so complicated? I'd gone from being a boring forty-something divorcee to being linked to a string of murders. Now, my detective ex-boyfriend thought I was a killer, the only other guy of interest didn't have an actual body, my bike had a taste for blood, and I kind of missed my boring Friday night pizza with The Jerk.

There had to be a way to fix this mess.

Let's see. The problem with Brayden seemed the easiest to fix. I wouldn't talk to him anymore.

What if he insisted? Or tried to take me in for questioning? Or retaliated because I wouldn't sleep with him?

What if he's not even a cop?

The sudden doubt planted a seed. Had I ever seen Brayden's badge? Nope. My dumb ass had never once asked to see one because I'd assumed he was telling the truth. After all, why else would he have been waiting for me to wake up that first time in the hospital? Yet not once had he asked me to go down to the station, nor had he ever taken a written statement.

Because wasn't I supposed to sign confessions or accusations?

He's a fake! Something I might be able to verify online.

Made me wonder what he got out of it, though. Probably one of those dudes who got off on being in a position of power over women. What if the Mahoney thing was part of his schtick? A shitty thing to do. Even shittier? I'd fallen for the act.

No more. I'd cut him out of my life, and if he harassed me, I'd press charges. And if he accused me of killing, well, I'd flip those tables and accuse right back.

Problem one solved.

Next one: Mahoney. Ghost or figment of my mind, didn't matter which category he fell into since he wasn't really a problem, other than the fact that I found myself falling in love. Pathetic. How to solve that? I needed to find a better balance between work and relaxation. I should meet and interact with people. Have sex with some real men.

Maybe I'd join a dating app. Wasn't there one just for fucking? Perhaps I'd start there. Worst-case scenario with Mahoney? If he refused to fade away, I'd see a doctor for some pills.

Which left me with the biggest issue: the murders linked to my bike.

A vehicle that had no registration number. No existence whatsoever. Only two living people knew of it: Brayden and me.

A ditched Brayden might snitch and tell the cops who owned the bike suspected in those killings. The cops would then show up with a search warrant. Could I hide the motorcycle? The junkyard had the room, but if the cops were thorough, they'd discover it.

Ditching it somewhere meant the risk of it being found. And, really, what if it *was* to blame for all the deaths? I couldn't let it kill any more people.

I had to get rid of it. No bike meant not only no evidence linking me to a crime, but it would also put a stop to the murder spree.

Lucky me, I had the machinery to demolish it. My metal compacter. Once I fixed it.

With the parts I'd ordered, I went to work, hesitating when I needed to enter the garage for my toolbox. I didn't know what I'd expected to see. The bike suddenly growling to life and running me down? Mahoney talking me out of it? He didn't appear, and the motorcycle sat in its spot, innocuous enough that I felt foolish.

Was I really going to blame a machine? How could I even think of destroying it?

Would I prefer to go to jail for a crime I didn't commit?

If I wanted to ride, I'd buy a new crotch rocket, one without any past history.

I lugged my tools to the compacter situated in one of the farthest corners of the yard. It seemed an odd spot until you saw the road running parallel to the fence and the oversized gate. An easy in and out that didn't require navigating any stacks. One created for trucks to cart away the metal.

As part of my learning process for the dump, I'd been looking into my options for disposing of the things that wasted space and served no use. Metal could be sold. The cleaner the bundles, the better the price. Meaning, I stripped vehicles of all the plastic, fabric, and glass that I could. Pity Canada hated incinerators. If I were located in Europe, I would have invested in one, and disposed of unrecyclable waste. At the same time, it would have generated electricity that I could have used to offset my use and sold the surplus back to the grid.

I didn't realize I had company until the bolt that wouldn't budge required my vise grips, and before I could reach for them, they dangled in front of my face.

"You'll regret destroying the bike."

Refusing to glance at Mahoney, I focused on tightening the bolt.

"Are you really going to pretend you can't hear me?" Mahoney growled in irritation.

I kept my gaze on the machine. "You're a figment of my imagination."

"Actually, the correct term is ghost. Which isn't easy for me to admit. Ever since you woke me, I've been trying to piece things together."

"How did I wake you?" Even as I asked, I knew. The horror movies gave me the answer. I'd bled on the frame of the bike. A bike he possessed.

"It was because you needed me."

"Why would a ghost care about a stranger?" I peeked at him.

"At the time, I was rescuing a damsel in distress," he admitted with a rueful grin.

I couldn't help a soft chuckle. "You are not a hero."

"Nope. But for you, I want to be."

"Ha, that's bullshit. The first time we met, you yelled at me."

"Because I was confused. I went from a deep, dreamless sleep to meeting you in what used to be my place."

"When you say you remember…" I hesitated.

"You want to know if I recall my death."

I nodded. Morbid, and yet I needed to know. "Was it a gang hit?"

"No. The detective on my case, the one I told you kept hounding me, he shot me four times in the chest and then once in the face."

My stomach clenched. "What was that detective's name?"

"Walker."

I gripped the wrench so hard, my knuckles turned white. "Brayden Walker?"

"No. His father, Silas. Fucker came to harass me about the folks dying in the city. When I wouldn't roll over and confess, he shot me in the garage. I bled out all over my ride. Things went dark for a while." His head dropped. "I woke up when I heard you crying out for help."

I could fill in the blanks to a certain point.

Silas Walker must have disposed of the body and hidden the bike covered in blood. What I didn't understand was Brayden's role.

"Brayden's dad shot you because he thought you were the Triclaw Killer?"

He nodded.

"If you're dead, then why is Brayden obsessed with you?"

The reply came from the man himself. "Because Mahoney killed my father."

CHAPTER 25

"BRAYDEN? WHAT ARE YOU DOING HERE?" Nerves strung tight, I kept a close eye on Brayden, currently walking—or was the more appropriate term rolling?—the wolf bike towards me. No longer the clean-cut guy I'd gotten to know, I didn't recognize this version dressed all in black, openly wearing a sidearm. Black cargo pants, tight, long-sleeved T-shirt. Over that, a Kevlar vest. Heavy, black boots and his gauntlets appeared to be of a thick gauge—armored in anticipation of battle.

"Why do you think I'm here, Allie?" He shook the motorcycle. "I told you to leave it buried. But you just had to bring the past back to life."

Mahoney sidled close. "Don't trust him."

"I don't," I muttered.

Brayden halted by the bulky frame of the compactor. "Have you finished with the repairs?"

How did he know I was working on it? Given his interest, I lied. "Not even close to done." I clung tightly to the socket wrench in my hand. Not as hefty as the pipe version, but would still do some damage if swung.

"Lying again. You seem to have made a habit of it. To be expected, I guess, given *his* influence." Brayden glanced at me, and the disdain shocked me.

I snapped, "You're one to talk about lying, *Detective*. I know you weren't assigned my case."

"That part might have been a fib, but I am a detective with the OPP."

"Really? Wonder what they'd think if they heard what you've been up to."

"Nothing, because you won't be talking to anyone about us." The confident smirk begged for a punch.

"Fucking smug bastard." Mahoney swung, and his fist went right through Brayden. The more terrifying thing? Brayden never even noticed. Didn't flinch or move.

Me, I gaped. Fuck. Guess I was on my own with Detective Crazy. "What do you want from me?"

"I want Mahoney."

"Mahoney's dead."

"I know he is. Where's his spirit?"

"Ghosts aren't real."

"Don't fucking lie to me. Where is he?"

My sassy reply? "Standing right behind you."

Brayden whirled and brandished his gun as if that would work against a ghost. "Where? I can't see him."

Mahoney's frustration pulled his lip into a snarl as none of his blows landed.

"He's right in front of you," I announced. "Looking pretty pissed."

"You don't seem surprised by his presence." The gun whirled to aim at me. "How long have you been communicating with Mahoney?"

"A while."

"How. Long?"

"Since the attack."

"And what has he said?"

"That he's innocent."

Brayden snorted. "And you believe him?"

"Why would a dead man lie?"

"To gain your trust so you'd lower your guard."

"Don't listen to him," Mahoney whispered behind me. "He's trying to get in your head."

"Why would a ghost need me to trust him?"

"How else would he possess your body?"

CHAPTER 26

MAYBE I SHOULDN'T HAVE LAUGHED. AFTER ALL, Brayden believed what he accused me of.

"I am not possessed."

"My surveillance says otherwise."

I blinked as I digested his words. "You've been spying on me?"

"Since you bought the place."

"Why would you even care?"

"My father died here."

I remember what he'd said upon arriving. "You said Mahoney killed him."

"Because he did."

"Mahoney says your dad shot him to death, so one of you is lying."

"Nope. Both statements are true." Brayden let go of the bike, which remained upright despite no kickstand. He put his hand on the lowered anvil of the compacter. "My dad parked the car with Mahoney's body in the compacter. Somehow, he got caught inside the vehicle when the machinery turned on. "

"Oh, fuck." I glanced at the wide crack through which rusty, crunchy metal and possibly other things peeked.

"Fuck is right. I knew I shouldn't have left him alone. My gut said something was wrong. But while Dad took care of the body, I got rid of the bike. On my way back, I heard the screams. It was too late by the time I reached him." Brayden's lips turned down.

"The fuck is lying," Mahoney insisted. "I remember what happened. He was the one who killed Ginny and framed my old gang. Daddy Walker discovered the truth, so Brayden got rid of him, too."

I glanced from Mahoney to Brayden. Who to believe? Who lied?

"Did you kill your father?" A blunt query to catch Brayden's reaction.

Instant suspicion. "Why would you ask that?" His expression cleared. "He's talking to you right now, isn't he?"

"He says he was being framed. By you.

That you're a killer. Your father found out, and you silenced him."

"Wow, now there's a web of lies."

"Did you?"

"How can you ask that?" Brayden shook his head, and his shoulders slumped. "I guess I shouldn't be surprised. From the sounds of it, he always did have a way with women."

In that moment, I became uncertain again. Brayden might be many things, but a murderer?

I eyed his strange attire. "You still haven't said why you're here and what you're doing with the bike."

"I'm here because Mahoney's spirit is still killing people." Brayden turned from the compacter to gesture to the bike. "I'm going to stop it once and for all."

"A ghost has no body. How can it kill?"

"By using someone else's hands." Brayden glanced at mine. "Tell me, Allie, how long have you been having blackouts?"

CHAPTER 27

THE INSINUATION ALMOST PUT ME ON MY ASS. "I'm not a killer."

"I know you're not. It's his fault." He glared at the motorcycle. "Once he's gone, you'll be fine."

"I..." I actually choked on what to say next because the idea of being possessed and murdering folks horrified.

Mahoney sputtered. "He's so fucking full of shit. Still trying to blame other people for his crimes."

I glanced at the man only I could see. "Swear. Swear to me you're the innocent guy here."

"Fucking right, I am. Your detective is a goddamned psycho."

That was all I needed to know. My gut said Mahoney spoke the truth. Brayden might sound convincing, but then again, being a psychopath meant that he believed every word he uttered.

Brayden half turned from me to slam the button that started the compactor. The grinding of metal as it moved after more than a decade proved jarring. It also hid my approach.

Before I could swing, a smell hit me, along with a wail. One long trapped that only now could escape. As the compactor retracted, I stared at the flattened carcass of a car which supposedly held two bodies.

Would it be soon become three? Brayden still hadn't indicated what he'd do to me.

He ignored the metal husk and dragged the bike atop it in the newly opened space. Mahoney tried in vain to pull it back out. His ghostly hands went right through it.

I found myself arguing to save it. "Destroying the bike won't help."

"Kill the host and the soul becomes untethered."

"And you know this how?"

Brayden cast me a short glance over his

shoulder. "Because I've been studying the afterlife."

"Why?"

"Because I wanted to be ready in case Mahoney returned. An evil like him doesn't easily die."

"What else do you know about ghosts?"

"That they require tethers to remain in this world and that a loose spirit requires a suitable vessel. Something with a connection to them when they were living. An object. A person." Brayden turned fully towards me. "Given what you've already done for him, I'm sorry for what I'm about to do."

The threat had me swinging. Brayden managed to block the blow, and the next, arm blocks that jarred my attempts to hurt him. All he did was defuse me. His cop training came in handy as he knocked the ratchet from my hands, grabbed my wrist, spun me, and before I could retaliate, had my hands ziptied behind my back.

Slick. And kind of scary because it put me at his mercy.

"Don't kill me." I wasn't above begging.

"I'm hoping I won't have to." He tugged me until I sat on the ground, with him crouching in front of me. "This next part is going to be hard, Allie. You need to focus on staying in control. If Mahoney senses weakness, he will dive in."

"What are you talking about?" I huffed as he headed for the compacter switch.

"Once I destroy the bike, Mahoney's spirit will look for a new place to hunker. I've got the mental fortitude to keep him out." Brayden tapped his temple. "You have to try really hard to do the same."

"And if he gets inside my head?"

"Then I'm really sorry."

The implication chilled me. "Brayden, listen to yourself. Possessed motorcycle. Body-jumping spirit. You're not thinking straight."

"There is nothing wrong with me, Allie. You're the one with a problem. The one who let him in because you didn't listen to me. But don't worry. I'm going to fix this."

"Brayden?" I injected a warning note.

"Be strong," he yelled as he started the compactor, and the anvil on top descended toward the motorcycle.

I knew better than to do something stupid like throw myself at the closing gap. A bike didn't merit me losing my life, yet tears rolled down my cheeks because Mahoney stood in front of it, his expression grave—as if resigned to his fate.

"I wish we could have had more time," Mahoney said with a soft smile.

"I don't want you to die. Again," I corrected at the end.

He glanced behind for a quick second as metal began to crunch. "Guess it's finally my time. Glad I got to meet— Ungh," he grunted as the bike frame began to compress.

"Mahoney," I whispered his name, seeing him fade before me. With each creak and snap of metal, I cringed. Until I screamed. "Stop, you're killing him."

"Good," was Brayden's reply. "Almost done. Guard your mind now."

A translucent Mahoney scowled. "Fucker. This isn't over."

The last thing he said as the bike crushed completely, and Mahoney disappeared. No fade. No last yell. Gone.

I uttered a wail, and Brayden stalked over and snapped, "Stop that."

"You killed him."

"You can't kill a ghost," Brayden argued.

"He was real to me," I muttered. Even if he

didn't have a body, Mahoney had a personality. What a shame the wrong person still lived.

Fingers snapped in front of my face. "Look at me. I want to see if he got inside." He gripped me by the chin, gentler than his tone would have indicated.

"What if he is? Then what? You going to crush me, too?"

His lips flattened. "No, that would be cruel. I care about you, Allie. I wish things could have gone differently. If only you'd been stronger."

He ran his knuckles down my cheek and I wanted to spit at him. Only I worried that like the last time I tried, it would end up slopping on my face. Hard to make a dramatic exit with goober rolling down the chin. "If I die, won't his spirit just find another body? We are in a junkyard."

"It's not that easy. He needs a personal tie to the person or object in question. A way in created by familiarity." He remained gentle even as he knocked my ankles out and lowered me to the ground.

"Stop this, Brayden. I thought we had a thing for each other." I could fake passion to live.

"We did, which is why this is hard for me to do. But I can't let my father and all those people die in vain. I promise to make it quick." He lifted his gun and aimed it at my head.

I literally looked down the barrel of his gun.

And that was when death swooped in, a thing of claws and fur, red eyes, and fury.

My baby, Blade.

CHAPTER 28

BLADE FOUND HIS BALLS LONG ENOUGH TO SAVE the day and headbutted Brayden so hard, the man flew away from my body, hit the compactor, and slumped to the ground.

Dead? I hoped not. Might be complicated to explain to the cops. Then again, maybe not with my hands tied behind my back. Even a cop would have to admit to something hinky going on. What about when Brayden woke, though? What would he say? Would he accuse me of being a killer?

It would be his word against mine. No evidence to tie me to the murders, despite what he claimed. With the bike gone, it would be hard to prove.

But what if I was wrong? The only way I'd be free and clear—

I turned my gaze from the unconscious body. No, I would not do that. Not even to save myself. As I shoved myself into a sitting position, my big, brave dog came to slurp me. I swore he knew I had no hands to defend myself.

Then again, I didn't really mind. I'd earned my slobbery kisses since Blade had saved me. I'd never make fun of his quirks again because when the moment called for it, he'd done the right thing and saved the maker of his bacon.

"Who's going to get a T-bone steak? A big one," I baby-talked, and Blade got so excited he peed a little in my lap. It was okay. I planned to toss out these pants anyhow. I leaned my head on his flank and murmured, "What are we going to do?"

The right thing, it turned out. After I sawed through the zip tie binding my hands and ordered my dog to sit on Brayden, I went through the detective's pockets.

The wallet coughed up his driver's license, badge, and a picture of me taken as I smiled at my dog in the yard. I pressed his fingerprint to his phone to unlock it and browsed through the contacts. He'd marked my number as his favorite and titled it: *Girlfriend.*

He'd yet to stir, and the purple bruising at his temple indicated a likely concussion—if he woke.

Given the strong probability, along with his evident obsession with me, I fabricated a fantastic story for the EMTs. The boyfriend and I were playing tag—you know, as a foreplay thing—when he tripped and fell. Simple, and me flustered enough that they bought it. I didn't even get a visit from the boys in dark blue about one of their own ending up in the hospital.

Just in case, though, I visited each day for the first two weeks of the coma. According to the doctors, he'd almost died twice. But each time, he'd rallied back.

The cranial bleed, his only real injury, healed, but his brain showed no signs of activity. If they didn't see anything soon, unless some unknown family member stepped forward, there would be a request to the courts to pull the plug.

While all this went on, I got rid of the evidence in my compactor. Wasn't all that hard, given I bundled the bike and smooshed car in with some other metal scrap and sold it. Just in case, though, I also scrubbed that compactor with bleach, then acid-washed the surface. Try and get some fucking DNA now. I covered my bases and waited.

The hospital advised me that they'd gotten court permission and would be taking Brayden off life support. Knowing that Brayden would die shortly, I visited one last time, sneaking Blade in with me. Okay, so I didn't sneak. I slapped a service dog vest on him and faked it. To Blade's credit, since his rescue of me, he'd been much braver but still just as smothering in bed. I remained less than impressed with his new obsession with crotch sniffing.

Not cool.

Upon entering Brayden's room, the soft beep of machines met me along with the still form of the man lying in the bed. One who'd tried to shoot me because he'd thought the ghost of a serial killer possessed me. How ironic that the detective had never once realized he'd been the one who needed to be taken down.

The murders had stopped the moment Brayden went unconscious. Soon, he'd die. The cycle of violence ended here.

Maybe. I had to admit a certain fascination with the killings. People online were clamoring for more vigilante justice. They wanted the scum taken from the streets. So did I. But I no longer had the bike to help me.

The doctor came in and offered me a nod. We'd already spoken. A nurse unhooked the machines and wheeled them out. Once they left, the room became silent.

Brayden's breaths turned shallow and far between. The end neared. I didn't feel like watching it. After all, there was a time I'd wanted this man inside my body.

Rising from his bedside, I didn't say good-bye, but my dog did, pouncing on the bed to bestow a tongue kiss on Brayden's lips.

Gross, but better him than me.

Over the next few days, I kept expecting to get a call from the hospital. *We're sorry to inform you...* To see something on the news. *Local detective dies while in the midst of a case.* How long could a body survive without machines feeding it? Surely, the internet would have some mention of the detective who'd passed away from an accident during freaky sex.

Instead, the dead man showed up at my door.

CHAPTER 29

UNTHINKING, I OPENED MY DOOR AT THE FIRST knock and then tried to slam it shut. Brayden wedged a foot in—obviously, not dead as hoped—and grunted. "Ow. Really, is that how we're saying hello these days, babycakes?"

"Go away! I don't want to see you."

"And yet, you were by my bedside each day."

"Waiting for you to die."

"Guess you're surprised to see me back."

I swung open the door to growl, "What do you want?"

"You."

"That chance sailed off a long time ago." As if I'd forget his attempt to murder me.

"Can't say as I blame you. Brayden was

253

rather gauche from the sounds of it. Don't worry, babycakes, I'll help you forget all about him."

That was the second time he'd said it. I angled my head. "What did you call me?"

"My sweet babycake. Did you miss me?"

"Something's different about you." It wasn't just his choice of clothing either: jeans, Sherpa-lined leather jacket, a cocky grin. Or his referring to himself in the third person. Disbelief smacked me. "Mahoney, is that you?"

"In the flesh. Just not mine." He grimaced down at the body. "The good detective liked his donuts a bit much. Nothing I can't fix in the gym, though."

"But how? The bike. It was crushed, and you were gone."

He shrugged. "Honestly, I'm not sure. All I know is I suddenly went from being part of the bike to dreaming I was a dog, and then I woke up."

"In Brayden's body?"

"Yeah. I'll admit, not exactly my first choice. Still, I guess I could have done worse."

"Worse how? The guy was a sadistic murderer." I had no doubt who the bad person was anymore. Not after everything Brayden had done.

"He might have been a killer, but he was never caught because he destroyed all the evidence."

"How can you be sure?"

"Because I went through his place. Hospital was kind enough to give me back his shit, including his keys, and one of the boys from the station drove me home."

"Wait, is this permanent?" I asked, confused because I'd gone from terror at seeing him to a slowly pulsing elation that Mahoney had returned. In a body I wouldn't mind touching.

"Seems to be. It's been three days now."

Three? I shoved him. "You've been in his body for three days and only just visited me now?"

"I wanted to make sure it would last before I came to see you. Kind of worried he'd shove me back out."

"I think you'll be fine. Brayden was brain dead. It's why the doctor pulled the plug. I guess because of your connection to each other, your ghost was able to slide in."

EVE LANGLAIS

"Sounds plausible, but I'm not crazy about it."

"Why not?"

"For one, my dick was way bigger. And I was taller."

"That guy is dead. And given the choice between your body now and a metal motorcycle, guess which I'd rather cuddle." I stepped closer, and he held his ground, looking down at me.

"Don't knock the bike, babycakes. Loved the way you used to straddle me," he purred, dragging me upwards towards his lips.

"I can think of a better way to straddle you," I teased, brushing my words against his lips.

"Show me."

It was the last thing he said before I finally got fucked. It started with a torrid kiss. We didn't make it to the bed. It happened right by that front door, with me pushed against the wall and him thrusting into me. The second bout happened in my bed, more slowly, with my climax making me scream loudly enough that I was glad I had no neighbors near.

Later that night, as we snuggled while a dejected dog lay across the foot of the bed, I

256

traced circles on his chest. "What are you going to do now with your new lease on life?"

"I'm thinking the good detective might be retiring."

"And what will he do with all that spare time?"

"There's an old DeLorean in the east corner I always meant to rebuild."

"Hmm. I don't know. There is a nice, '72 Ford Baja Bronco I've been eyeing."

"Maybe I can convince you?" he purred before getting under those sheets between my legs.

I screamed, "Yes," as I came. Then again and again. Because, apparently, I'd entered my insatiable years.

Blame the steel wolf between my thighs.

EPILOGUE

LIFE IN THE FLESH PROVED MORE MARVELOUS than Mahoney recalled, although he really had to do something about the name situation. Every time someone called him Detective Walker, he almost shot them.

Killian "Junkdog" Mahoney wouldn't complain though because he'd gotten a second chance. This time, he wouldn't fuck it up. He'd already started with the love of an epic woman. Meeting her as a ghost had been tough. Especially since she'd been dating another man.

It was kind of ironic that the guy who'd never slept with her fucked her every night now. And morning. Also midday. He had a decade to make up for.

Thinking of Allie brought her in sight. She entered the garage as she said goodbye to someone on the phone.

"Well, that was fucked up." She chewed her lower lip with an intentness that reminded him of how she looked when she sucked his cock. Perfect.

And mine.

"What's wrong?" he asked, and could it be solved by sex?

Her nose wrinkled. "I had the weirdest conversation with Sonja."

"Sonja being?" he prompted.

"The Jerk's new wife. Widow, actually. Apparently, Ashton, my ex, died in a freak accident. Something about the lawnmower turning murder machine and chopping him to pieces."

Mahoney winced. "Ouch."

"Not as painful as listening to Sonja losing her shit on the phone. Demanding I take custody of his baby."

"Wait, what?" He didn't have to feign confusion.

"Seems like Sonja doesn't want to be a single mother. She thinks because I was with The Jerk for so long, I should take his kid. Raise his legacy. Said I owed it to him."

He snorted. "Oh, boy."

Allie grinned. "Right? Of all the people to ask. As you might guess, I told her she could kindly fuck off. Then I told her that with him dead, and her admitting that I'd put in more years than she had, I'd be coming after his half of the assets."

"Isn't she his wife?"

"Yes. However, I took care of all the paperwork during our marriage. Benefits, life insurance. Even his will." Allie shrugged. "Pretty sure he never changed the beneficiary's name on any of those. So, legally, it's all mine. Not that I'll keep it. I'll have a lawyer look into setting up a trust managed by someone who will make sure Sonja can't spend it all before the kid can inherit."

"Look at you doing good."

"More like pissing off Sonja the best way I know how."

He barked a chuckle. "So evil. Love it."

"Not as evil as a lawnmower suddenly turning on its owner." Allie's gaze narrowed on him. "Sonja said it was as if it were possessed."

"Imagine that," he whispered, dropping a kiss on her lips.

"Weren't you in Southern Ontario a few days ago, picking up those parts?"

"Yup." No point in denying it. He wouldn't ever lie to Allie. "Lawnmowers are dangerous."

To which she smirked. "The Jerk never *was* good with power tools. I assume you left no link?" Asked matter-of-factly. She'd come to grips with the truth when she'd seen the videos Brayden had taken of her, leaving the junkyard on the bike, hair streaming, face clearly visible. The ex-detective even had her on record killing the night before Mahoney's epic chopper was destroyed. Looking fierce in her leather and red cape, grinning as she took out the scourge of society.

Mahoney had shown her everything the departed detective had stored in the cloud, knowing that he took a risk. A gamble that'd paid off. Allie had turned to him and said, *"I know I should feel guilty about it, but I don't. I made the world a safer place."*

"We're in the clear, babycakes."

"Good." Then she said the sexiest thing imaginable. "The crime in this area is getting bad. Might be a good night for a ride. What do you say, steel wolf?"

Fuck, yeah, he wanted to ride. First against the wall with her legs around his waist, and her screaming in climax. Then with her geared up in her leather, perched on the back of his new motorcycle. Not much to look at yet, but he'd been working on acquiring parts for the upgrade. The most important thing for the moment was that it came with a seat for two.

And a pair of fenders, more red than black, reclaimed from the compacter.

Yet another story inspired by a cover. A rollicking ride that I hope you loved. And isn't it fun seeing a mature heroine getting her adventure and happily ever after?

FOR MORE EVE LANGLAIS BOOKS VISIT EVELANGLAIS.COM

CPSIA information can be obtained
at www.ICGtesting.com
Printed in the USA
BVHW070114020822
643555BV00009B/151

9 781773 843049